# The Celtic Locket Legacy

## Book 2: Beth Riley, the Orphan

Adda Leah Davis

ISBN: 978-1-959700-20-3

## Acknowledgments

I first wish to state that my ability to write is my gift from my almighty God and I hope that I never fail to give him praise and thanks for that gift. God is the author and the finisher of my faith and my ability to string words together in such a fashion as to offer entertainment to my readers.

In each book that I complete, I find myself remembering all the wonderful people who knowingly or unknowingly contributed to the story. One person who did more on this book than anyone else is my great-niece, Jill Dunkel of Michigan. She went through the entire book several times and was so much help in keeping me from rambling, making grammatical errors, and helping me make my story clear to my readers. Thanks, Jill, for your advice and help.

Hubert Brewster and his wonderful wife, Barbara, have been so encouraging and supportive of my work that I made Hugh a lawyer in this book. I know that isn't his field of expertise, but he could probably do that too, since he has accomplished so much in his life. Thanks, Barbara and Hugh for your friendship and support.

Jerry Scarberry sent me a book about Mountain Mission School which was so helpful in writing this book. I certainly wish to let Jerry and his wife Martha know how much I appreciate their friendship and encouragement.

Since Victoria Fletcher, owner of Hoot Books Publishing is my publisher and great friend, she deserves double credit for the many ways in which she has helped me. Anyone wishing to have a book published should look first at the Hoot Books Publishing website. Once they see what is offered, I think their search will be over.

# AN ORPHAN'S PLIGHT

The sun is bright and shining and I shouldn't be sad.
Cheerful bird songs should make everyone glad.
For I have plenty of food and a roof o'er my head
and I know I have much more than many folks have.
But I feel so alone with no mommy or dad.

Here, I'm an orphan just like all my friends
who lives in this place which gathered me in.
A great place of shelter, safety, and care.
I'm fed, I'm clothed, and I'm free from fear.
But I'm still alone with no mommy or dad.

I've learned to do chores and I go to school.
And here I am taught about "The Golden Rule."
Which helps me to live as a family should.
And I've had lots of training to make my life good,
but I'm still alone with no mommy or dad.

I've adapted to life's struggles and obeyed the commands
dealt out in the school's efforts to rear "helping hands."
I'm taught to be helpful to all those in need.
Not to just talk the talk, but to do the deed.
But I'm still alone with no mommy or dad.

Then God paid me a visit, and everything changed.
What a marvelous blessing that visit became.
Now I'm a child of the Savior and I'm where I belong.
I'm in his family of children and no longer alone
because God opened his arms and welcomed me Home.

# BETH RILEY, THE ORPHAN

***Find a place inside where there is joy, and the joy will burn out the pain." ~Joseph Campbell***

## CHAPTER 1

*I can't go to sleep or that man will come and get Mommy,* thought Beth Riley, as again her head fell back against the seat.

Beth lived in terror that the man called Jesus would come and take her mommy away as he had her daddy.

The four-year-old daughter of James and Marcie Riley of Pittsburgh, Pennsylvania was on a train for the first time. Beth, her mother, and a nurse were riding a train bound for Grundy, Virginia.

"I don't want to go to sleep, Mommy," mumbled Beth Riley, as she raised her head again to look at her mother.

The clickety-clack of the train wheels became a monotonous drone and Beth couldn't keep her eyes open.

When Alice Turpin said her daddy was dead, Beth's life had become a daytime nightmare. She was afraid to sleep or leave her mommy's side, and food seemed to lodge in her throat.

After that first week's wild bouts of screaming, Beth became a somber wraith hovering around her mommy like a guardian angel. *I guess Mommy's too sick to help me stop that man,* thought Beth since her mother only spoke to tell Beth to eat, bathe, or go to bed.

Beth did each thing she was told to do, except go to bed. Instead, she had silently crept onto the sofa every night to be beside her mommy who now slept in her recliner chair.

On this long two-day train ride, she had fought to stay awake, even though the nurse scolded her constantly. "Lay down on this cushion, Beth. Your mommy needs to rest and you're keeping her awake."

Beth didn't believe the nurse, but she obediently lay back against the cushion refusing to close her eyes. The repeating noise of the train was so monotonous that she eventually sank into a restless slumber, but soon jerked herself upright again.

She looked at her mother with wide worried eyes and whispered, "I'm really, really trying to stay awake, Mommy. You're sick, and I can't let him take you. If I go to sleep, he will come." She reached out to touch her mother's hand, but the nurse pushed her hand away.

"Don't bother your mother, Beth," scolded the nurse, who looked very sleepy herself.

Being four years old didn't help her to understand why her mommy coughed so much. Neither did she understand why they were taking this long train ride. The only thing she knew was that her daddy had not come home from work one evening and things had not been the same since.

Alice Turpin had said, "Your Daddy is dead, Little Beth. He won't be coming back anymore." This led to the state Beth was living in now.

"Your daddy has gone to heaven to be with Jesus," explained her mother, over and over, between her bouts of crying and coughing.

Once the screaming had subsided, Beth said, "Daddy loved me and you, Mommy. Why did he leave us to live with somebody we don't even know?"

Beth's mother was shocked that her daughter would think like that about Jesus, but she felt too tired and ill to even try to explain. Instead, she only hugged Beth and said she would explain later, but she never did.

A very tired and bewildered Beth sat in the noisy train and tried to remember everything that happened, but there was so much she didn't know or understand.

Beth recalled that she wasn't awake that day when her dad went to work, but she was awake when he didn't come home that evening.

That day, Beth had fixed cereal for herself and her mother. She was so proud when she climbed on the counter and got the cereal box and the bowls down.

"See, Mommy, I am a big help. Daddy said for me to help you all I could, and I am," stated Beth proudly.

Marcie Riley, who at one time would have been petrified with fright, only gasped in surprise, and then smiled when she saw that Beth was safely on the floor again. She also sat quietly at lunch, allowed Beth to bring bread, lunchmeat, and mayonnaise to the table, and put together two sandwiches. Marcie didn't feel like eating but she succeeded in eating half of her sandwich since Beth expected her to.

Beth's parents, Jamie and Marcie Riley, had made a decision about something important, which would be a big surprise, or so they told Beth. She waited each day in expectancy for this big surprise.

Their clothes were packed in suitcases and trunks and Marcie slept or sat in her favorite reclining chair, waiting for the end of the week. She was trying to conserve all her energy for what they planned to do.

After Jamie left for work that day, Marcie didn't even try to get dressed. She bathed but still wore her soft fluffy blue robe. In this attire, she answered the door at five o'clock that evening to find a strange man standing on the stoop.

Beth was playing quietly in the bedroom, but hearing a plopping sound, she ran to the living room to find her mother on the floor and a strange man bent over her. Beth went barreling into the man, pummeling him with her small fists, and screaming.

"Don't you hurt my mommy?"

The man ignored Beth and scooped Marcie into his arms to deposit her on the sofa against the living room wall. He then turned to Beth.

"Your mommy fainted, Honey. I wasn't trying to hurt her."

Beth stopped screaming and gulped, "Oh! I heard her fall. Who are you?" Before the man could explain anything, Alice Turpin, their next-door neighbor, came panting through the door.

"What's happened here? Who are you and what are you doing here? Don't you know Mrs. Riley is too ill to have people calling on her?" demanded Alice.

"I'm Charles Merman, the President of Pittsburgh Steel Number Three," said the man as he put out his hand.

Alice shook his hand, as she stood gaping as if in shock. Suddenly she realized what his visit may mean and turned to Beth. "Beth, will you go over to my house and tell Flora to call the doctor?"

"Our phone works, Aunt Alice. Call the doctor on our phone."

"Beth, I need Flora to come over here

anyway. So, you go and tell her to call the doctor and then bring you back over here."

Seeing Beth's obstinate frown, Alice gave her a pleading look. "Please, Little Beth."

"The doctor will help Mommy, won't he, Aunt Alice?" asked Beth as she looked fearfully at her mother.

At Alice's nod, Beth ran out the door and down the steps as fast as her four-year-old legs would carry her. Flora did what she was told, but asked questions, to which Beth had no answers.

"I don't know, Flora. I was playing in my room, and I heard Mommy fall. I ran into the living room and a man was there. He put Mommy on the sofa and now she is asleep and won't wake up."

After the call was made, Flora took Beth's hand and together they walked back to Beth's house. There they found the doctor working with Marcie Riley, who was now sitting up but crying loudly. The strange man, Mr. Merman, was talking quietly to Alice Turpin in the kitchen.

Beth went to sit by her mother. Marcie Riley put her arms around Beth and clutched her tightly to her side. Beth sat looking at the doctor who was putting things into a black bag that sat on the couch beside her mother.

"Mommy's cough makes her sick, but

she'll get better. Won't she, Doctor?" Beth asked in a trembling voice.

The doctor looked down into the small round face with such large troubled brown eyes and swallowed. "I gave your mother some medicine that will make her sleep. She needs to rest. She should feel some better, but she needs to rest for a while." He then picked up his bag and went into the kitchen again.

Beth stayed huddled beside her mother until Alice Turpin came in and said, "Beth, honey you go in the kitchen with Flora and help her fix something to eat. Your mommy needs to eat and then go to sleep. I'll get her into bed and then she can have her supper in bed."

"Mommy and I always eat with Daddy. We'll just wait for him. He'll be home soon and then we can all eat."

Beth looked startled when her mother began to cry harder and start coughing again.

The doctor hurried back in and motioned for Beth to be taken into the kitchen as he opened his bag.

Alice Turpin took Beth's hand and said, "Come on, Honey, let's go in the kitchen and let the doctor help your mother." Beth stumbled along with her, looking back at her mother.

## CHAPTER 2

When it kept getting later and Jamie Riley didn't appear, Beth went to the door every few minutes until Alice Turpin said, "Your daddy isn't coming home this evening."

"Why?" asked Beth, but when she saw tears in Alice Turpin's eyes, she began to cry herself.

"Where's my Daddy? I want my Daddy! I want my Daddy!" she was now screaming. Beth felt something was not right but didn't know what it was.

"Your daddy is just held up at work, Beth," Alice explained over and over since Marcie had told her not to tell Beth anything. The next morning Jamie Riley still hadn't shown up and Beth's mother did not get out of bed. She lay looking off into space.

Alice Turpin came early the next morning. She fixed breakfast, but Marcie said she couldn't eat. Neither did she want to get out of bed.

"Mommy, you'll want to be up and dressed when Daddy gets here. Remember the big surprise is supposed to be this week." Beth ran first to the window and then back to her mother.

"Daddy will be here soon, Mommy, and Aunt Alice cooked breakfast for us."

Beth stood giving her mother such a pleading look that Marcie finally got out of bed.

She didn't dress though. She only donned her long blue robe and came to the table.

"Marcie, I'll run back to the house while you eat, but I'll be back in a little bit." Marcie nodded at Alice and smiled, but Beth said, "Thanks, Aunt Alice."

Alice came back at noon, bringing lunch with her. When she saw the pale and weepy Beth, she gathered Beth to her ample bosom. Alice's intent was to give a comforting hug, but Beth didn't like it. She felt suffocated in Alice's arms and struggled to get away and went back to her mother.

"Mommy, why are you sitting in daddy's chair?" asked Beth when her mother curled up in the matching chair to her recliner, which was Jamie Riley's usual seat. Snuggled closely in the chair, Marcie Riley sat looking at Jamie's picture and cried between spells of coughing.

After lunch, Beth kept running to look out the window. When the clock showed it to be four o'clock, she turned from the window once again. "Mommy, why is Daddy staying at work so long? He stayed all last night and now he is staying all day, too." Beth ran to the phone.

"What's the number to that Pittsburgh Steel place? I'm going to call my daddy."

"No, Beth. You can't call your daddy. They would get really upset," said Marcie and started crying and coughing again so Beth put down the phone and went to the kitchen as Alice again came with their food.

Beth still went to the window and stood staring as if willing her daddy to come down the street. Finally, since she didn't want her mother to start coughing again, she agreed to go to bed.

When Beth awoke the next morning, her daddy was still not home, and she knew something was different.

"Why hasn't Daddy come home, Mommy?" Beth stood by her mother's bedside waiting expectantly. When she only received a stricken look from her mother, she became almost hysterical.

Her screams could be heard on the street. "I want my Daddy. I want my Daddy."

Alice heard her through the door and hurried inside.

"Beth, that's not going to make your daddy come home and you are making your mother sick. Stop that screaming."

"I want my Daddy to come home. Why doesn't he come home?"

Alice was trying to help Marcie who was coughing, weeping, and trembling, and the screams were driving her to distraction.

"Stop that screaming. Your daddy can't come home. There was an accident. Your daddy was killed. He's dead, Beth."

Alice wasn't prepared for Beth's

onslaught and fell on the bed, as Beth, like a small bombshell, ran at her, pushing, kicking, and slapping with her small hands and feet while screaming, "No, no, no. My daddy is not dead. He is not."

Marcie jerked herself up to a sitting position, and said, "Beth, stop that. It is not your Aunt Alice's fault."

Beth stopped instantly and ran to her mother sobbing, "Mommy, she's saying my daddy is dead?"

Marcie pushed her feet off the bed and dropped to her knees, with Alice's help, and pulled Beth into her arms.

"Beth, Honey, there was an accident at the steel mill where your daddy worked. Several men were hurt but your daddy was killed."

Beth's large brown eyes glared and then lost focus as she slipped from her mother's arms and sank silently to the floor. Marcie started screaming but stopped when her cough started again.

Alice helped her to her feet and into a chair then picked up Beth and carried her to the living room sofa. She placed Beth on the sofa and went back to help Marcie. As soon as Alice had Marcie settled in a chair, she got a wet washcloth and began to wash Beth's face.

The outside door opened and Alice's daughter, Flora, came seeking her mother,

"Mom." Alice Turpin didn't even turn around as she said, "Call the doctor, Flora. Beth is out cold."

Beth opened her eyes but stared unseeing. That was how the doctor found her when he walked in. Marcie Riley was crying and coughing so badly that the doctor gave her some medicine to calm her before he worked with Beth.

"What brought this on? I know she has been crying but something must have happened to cause this kind of trauma," said the doctor looking at Alice.

"Mom told her that her daddy was dead," blurted Flora and Alice gave her a malevolent glare.

"She was worrying us all to death, crying, running to the door, and climbing up to the window. My legs were almost run off trying to take care of her mother and see to the things Mr. Merman told me to do here. I have my own house to care for, and I couldn't get her to stop screaming or listen to reason. I just blurted it out before I thought, I reckon," said Alice contritely.

The doctor washed Beth's face and she opened her eyes. "That's cold. Mommy washes me with warm water."

"How do you feel?"

Beth looked around and when she saw

Alice she sat up and glared at her. “Why did you lie to me? My daddy is not dead.”

Alice looked as if she too was ready to cry. “I’m so sorry, Beth, but your Daddy was killed in an accident. You know, like the man that was hit by that car last year.”

“But my dad was at work. There are no cars at that place,” said Beth as if she was reasonable.

The doctor sat down beside Beth on the sofa. “Beth, there was a belt that hauled steel to the furnace, and it broke. A piece of steel fell on your daddy,” he explained and was surprised when Beth jumped from the sofa and ran to the window screaming, “No! No! No! Daddy, Daddy, I want my daddy.”

Beth didn’t even notice when the doctor slipped the needle into her arm. He picked her up and placed her back on the sofa and she stopped crying and went to sleep.

“I’ve given her something to calm her. She will sleep for several hours. I think she’ll be all right, but I’ll leave some medicine. If she cries and you can’t get her to stop, give her a half teaspoon every six hours.” The doctor checked Marcie again and then left saying that he would be back that evening.

“I’d like to stay over here doctor, but I have other kids at home and my old man will want his supper. Can you get a nurse or somebody to come and stay? They don't need to be alone," said Alice who seemed worn out herself.

An hour later, Mr. Merman arrived with Ms. Ethel Ross, a private nurse who was to stay with Marcie and Beth until some other arrangement could be made.

# CHAPTER 3

Several days passed and both Beth and her mother grew steadily weaker. Mr. Merman came one night and he, Alice Turpin, the nurse, and Marcie Riley talked for a long time.

The next morning, Flora stayed with Beth while Aunt Alice went with her mommy and Mr. Merman to arrange the funeral. "What is a funeral?" asked Beth, but Flora just shrugged her shoulders as if she didn't know the answer.

"Your mother will explain it when she comes home," said Flora and tried to change the subject.

When Aunt Alice and her mother returned, Beth met her at the door. "What is a funeral, Mommy?" Flora said you went to arrange one.

Aunt Alice gave Flora a hard look but ignored Beth. Marcie Riley was having trouble walking and Aunt Alice was helping her. Beth stood watching as her mother was finally on the sofa lying back against the cushions.

"A funeral must be hard to do. It's made Mommy sick, hasn't it?" Beth went to stand by the sofa and reached out to touch her mother's forehead.

"Do you have a temperature, Mommy? You need some cold lemonade. That will make you better, won't it?"

Beth looked up, "Aunt Alice, will you

make Mommy some lemonade?"

"No, Beth, it won't make your Mommy better. She needs to lie back and be quiet. You go in the other room to play and let your Mommy rest."

Two days later Flora helped Beth dress in her best clothes and then helped a much weaker Marcie Riley dress in a new black dress.

"Where are we going, Mommy?" asked Beth since they were dressed so nicely.

"You're going for a ride in a bright shiny car," said Flora, as she tweaked the blue straw hat she had placed on Beth's head.

Beth looked out the window and saw that a shiny, black car had stopped in front of their house. Charles Merman came to the door and soon Beth and her mother were inside the car heading into town.

They stopped at a large building that Beth thought was a church, even though she had never been to any church.

Later, she remembered the day she and her Mommy and Daddy picnicked down by the river. Her daddy was lying back on the grass with his head in her mommy's lap.

"Marcie, you know we should take Beth to some church, don't you?" her dad had questioned.

"When she gets big enough, we will let her decide, and then we'll take her, or rather I will take her because I'm sure she will be a Presbyterian," replied her mother.

"She'd do better in a Catholic school, Marcie. I went to a Catholic school. They have good discipline, and the children learn more. The Sisters let you know right off about discipline," said her daddy as he sat up and laughed.

"I think Sister Mary Agnes got tired of cracking my knuckles with her ruler, and finally just gave up. I remember singing 'The Wearin' of the Green' too loud."

Beth asked, "What's a Catholic? I don't want to be cracked on the knuckles."

Marcie and Jamie laughed and hugged her close between them. "Let's not worry about that now Beth. You have a while yet before we need to worry about you going to school. Beth shook her head and went back to remembering what happened after her daddy died.

She remembered sitting beside her mother with Mr. Merman in the black shiny car as they rode to the big building with a cross above its door. When the car stopped, Beth and her mother were escorted from the car and taken inside the building.

Mr. Merman held her mother's arm on one side leaving her hand free to hold Beth's hand on the other side. Together they walked through a long aisle to the front of the building.

They stopped in front of a long white box with handles that rested on a covered table.

Aunt Alice Turpin and Flora were there also, and Alice took Mr. Merman's place beside Marcie and Flora took the other side holding Beth's hand.

Mr. Merman had stepped back but said, "Mrs. Riley, do you want me to lift your daughter so she can see."

Marcie hesitated and then started coughing. Unable to speak, she nodded her head and Mr. Merman said, "Here Beth, let me lift you up so you can see."

He lifted Beth in his arms until she could see inside the box.

"Daddy! What are you doing sleeping here? You didn't come to supper because you went to sleep, didn't you?" she scolded as she wriggled to get close. "Open your eyes. It's morning time, now. People don't sleep in the mornings."

Mr. Merman pulled her back from the casket and cuddled her close in his arms, as he said, "No Dear, your daddy can't wake up. He is not asleep."

He looked around helplessly for aid or support from someone. Not seeing any he asked, "Do you remember me telling you about the accident at the place where your daddy worked, and that he was hurt very badly?"

Beth nodded with a questioning look and Mr. Merman said, "So, now he is asleep and can't be with us anymore."

With her eyes big in her small face she said, "But, Daddy is right there. I can wake him up. He loves me and Mommy. He wants to be with us."

She tried to wriggle out of Mr. Merman's arms, but he held her closer.

"Let me go," Beth ordered. "Daddy always wakes up for me."

When Mr. Merman held her more firmly, Beth began to kick and scream.

"I want my daddy. I can wake him up." Mr. Merman looked beseechingly at Alice Turpin, and she left Marcie to Flora's care, and came to his aid.

"Here, Beth, let me hold you. You need to stop screaming and kicking or you'll make your mommy start coughing again," cautioned Alice taking Beth gently into her arms.

Marcie was standing, with Flora's help, by the side of the casket. She had been crying softly, but she started coughing and Alice motioned for Flora to help her toward the first row of seats.

Not wanting to make her mommy cough, Beth tried to control herself, but she couldn't stop crying. However, she watched in fascination as a man, in a fancy kind of robe came in and stood on a throne above her daddy.

"Who is that?" asked Beth in a whisper to Alice. "Is he Jesus?"

"Shh. Be quiet. Please, Beth," begged Alice, and Beth sagged in Alice's arms and tried to listen. The man talked about heaven and Jesus and how much Jesus loved her daddy.

*He does not love my daddy. My daddy didn't ever want to go to any other place except that pretty, green place called Ireland, but he wanted me and Mommy to go with him. I love my daddy and I want him to wake up*, she thought, and suddenly jumped from Alice's arms and rushed to the casket. She tried to climb up onto the casket, but Mr. Merman caught her up in his arms. Kicking and screaming, she was carried from the building.

Mr. Merman put her in the car beside her mother, and they rode behind a line of cars to a place called a cemetery, crying all the way.

When the car stopped, they got out, and Beth ran to her mother. "Mommy, where are we? I don't like this place."

Marcie didn't speak or move, and Beth stood beside her with Mr. Merman watching. Shocked, Beth watched in wide-eyed horror as several men took the box with her daddy inside and put it down in a big hole in the ground.

As the box was lowered into the hole, Beth tried to break away from Mr. Merman, but she could not free herself. She struggled as she screamed, "Daddy, Daddy," in a piercing shriek until she lost consciousness.

Marcie was crying and coughing and at Beth's screams, she too sagged to the ground. One of the men attending the funeral picked her up and with Flora's help put both Beth and her mommy back into the car.

# CHAPTER 4

The next weeks were days of moping around the house and nightmarish nights from which Beth awoke screaming, "Daddy, Daddy. I want my daddy."

Her mother's cough got worse. She wasn't eating and she seemed to always be awake. Even when Beth awoke from one of her nightmares, her mother was awake and the nurse that Mr. Merman had sent would be there with her.

Marcie tried to talk to Beth. "Honey, your daddy was killed in an accident at the Steel Mill where he worked. He is dead and he won't be back to us. He has gone to be with Jesus."

"But, Mommy, he loved me and you best. He said he did," cried Beth. "My daddy didn't go to be with Jesus. He's up there at that place called cemetery. He's in a hole and he can't get out if we don't help him."

"Beth, Honey, please try to understand. Daddy doesn't know what happened, for his spirit has gone to be with Jesus," Marcie explained wearily.

Beth did not understand, but Ethel, the nurse had explained that her mother was sick and her asking questions made her mother feel worse, so she didn't ask any more questions. However, she knew that she certainly didn't love this Jesus person. He took her daddy away.

A month after the funeral, Ethel and Aunt Alice packed all their things and a taxi took Beth, her mother, and Ethel, the nurse, to a place with lots and lots of trains. A man wearing a cap on his head helped them into the train, and they were taken to a room inside one of the little houses. Ethel said this was a car.

"No, it isn't. A car has wheels and runs on the street," said Beth. Ethel gave her a strange look while continuing to help Marcie get settled.

Soon the engine started, and the train whistled shrilly. Beth covered her ears. The whistling stopped and the train began to move. Beth stood on her feet in the seat and watched out the window as they left Pittsburgh behind.

They rode the train all day and night. Beth was tired, sleepy, and very hungry. Marcie coughed all night and when morning came, she again began spitting into the trash can; that yucky stuff that made Beth feel sick when she once saw it. The nurse quickly came to her mother's aid, and brought her some thick pads, to shield her clothing from any stray sputum, along with a box of tissues.

Finally, someone yelled, "All out for Grundy" and Marcie pulled herself up, with Ethel's help, and holding a tissue over her mouth she turned to Beth.

"Let's go, Beth. This is where we get off," said Marcie taking Beth's hand. Ethel and the conductor had to help them from the train. Ethel stood, holding Marcie erect, while a man ordered a taxi for them.

"We need to go to Mountain Mission School," said Marcie between shuddering coughs. Beth had heard about this school, but she had not been in on the conversations or plans that her parents had made due to Marcie's illness. She had only been told that she and her mother would have to do some things that they may not want to do but were necessary since her daddy was no longer with them. Now, she supposed that this trip was one of those unwanted things, but she didn't like it.

She watched fearfully as Ethel whispered softly to the conductor for a few minutes. Beth could not hear because of the hissing noises and so many people were talking in loud voices. Also, the train was huffing and puffing, and its bell was clanging.

The conductor talked to the taxi driver when he arrived, and then helped the three of them inside the taxi. First, they were driven across the railroad tracks and across a bridge then up this narrow, paved road which ran beside a river. Finally, they turned up a hill beside a big brown water wheel with water splashing and shining as the wheel turned over and over. Beth couldn't take her eyes off that constantly moving water as it splashed over the wheel. *It makes me feel safe, or something,* she thought when it first came into view.

Something about the wheel with the water washing over it in sparkling splashes seemed to ease some of the heaviness in Beth's heart. She watched it until the car went slowly up and around a little curve and the wheel was lost from view. The road continued around and up the hill to a big house at the top.

Ethel tipped the driver after he had helped them out. He carried Beth's bags up to the house while Ethel helped Marcie.

"Where are your bags, Mommy? The man didn't get your bags," said Beth anxiously.

"He'll bring mine later, Honey," explained Marcie as she turned to the taxi driver.

"Will you wait for a few minutes, please? We won't be too long, I don't think," said Marcie, and at the driver's nod, they went up some steps and into a building.

A large, bald man with glasses was standing by a row of windows that looked out over a green lawn.

The man turned as they went in, and Marcie said, "I'm Mrs. James Riley, from Pittsburgh who called you last week and this is my daughter, Bridget Elizabeth Riley."

Marcie turned to the nurse and said, "This is Ethel Ross, a nurse, who traveled with us."

The man smiled and came to meet them.

"I'm Wilbur Wright, the director. He pulled out two chairs and said, "You ladies have a seat, Mrs. Riley, and I'll get someone to take . . . What is your daughter called, I mean what do you call her?" he asked.

"Beth," replied Marcie as a short plump woman with her brown hair done up in a bun at the back of her head came into the room.

"Mrs. Riley, this is Mrs. Collins, the mother supervisor for the little ones. She'll take Beth to the bathroom and get her some cookies while we talk. Is that all right?" asked Mr. Wright and smiled at Marcie's nod of approval.

Beth clung to her mother until Marcie gave her a hug and rasped, "Go with the nice lady, Beth. I know you need to use the bathroom."

Beth was hungry and very puzzled, but Mommy had told her that now they would have to do things they did not want to do because her daddy couldn't come back. Beth knew where he was, though, but mommy said he still couldn't come back.

Beth went with Mrs. Collins, looking back at her mommy until the door closed.

"Where am I going? I want to stay with Mommy. She says that I can't go to that hospital with her," said Beth trying hard not to cry.

Mrs. Collins squeezed the hand she held as she kept walking down a long hall with a stairway at the end. As they started to climb a set of stairs, she stopped.

"Beth, I want to show you where twelve other little girls have their beds, their clothes, and their toys. It's a long room and it's called a dormitory. I sleep in a little room just outside the door of that long room. You can come to me when you feel bad or have any kind of problem. I'll take care of you until your mommy comes back for you," promised Mrs. Collins who had stooped to Beth's level and looked at her with a kind smile.

Beth threw her arms around Mrs. Collins. "I'm scared. I don't know anybody, and nobody knows me either. My daddy is in a big box in the ground and now my mommy is sick."

Mrs. Collins unclasped Beth's arms and pushed her back so that she could see Beth's face. "Listen Bethy . . . may I call you Bethy?"

Beth nodded as tears trickled down her cheeks. Mrs. Collins continued. "Bethy, all the other girls that are here are just like you. Some of these girls have never seen their mother or daddy but they are happy here.

"Sometimes, children must do things they don't want to do. This is one of those things, so please try to accept it and hope that your mommy will be better soon. You are better off than some of these girls . . . you do have a mommy," explained Mrs. Collins.

Beth again remembered her mother, saying when her daddy didn't come back from work, that now they would have to do things they did not want to do. She looked at Mrs. Collins, who had just said the same thing, and Beth thought, *If I don't like this place, I'll still have this kind person to help me.*

Mrs. Collins took Beth's hand and led her to a large bathroom and then into another room where there were cookies on a table and milk in a refrigerator. Mrs. Collins soon fixed a plate with two cookies and poured a glass of milk.

"Here, Bethy, drink this milk with your cookies. We make the cookies here and having them with milk makes them so much better."

Beth liked the cookies and when she was finished, they went into another room full of tables and games with pretty pictures of Mother Goose on the walls. Beth was enchanted to see her storybook friends so lifelike on the walls. She slowly went around the walls softly touching and patting the rabbits and the chicks and almost forgot about how puzzled and scared she was.

Then a boy came into the room. "Mr. Wright wants you in the office," he said with a smile at Beth.

"What's your name?" he asked.

Beth didn't answer but Mrs. Collins said, "This is Beth Riley, Jimmy," she has come to live with us until her mother gets better."

# CHAPTER 5

They went back to the room where her mother was, and Beth saw that her mother was still crying. Her eyes and face were red and puffy.

She ran to her mother. "Is your cough worse, Mommy?" asked Beth since Marcie seemed to be having trouble breathing.

"Mommy, you didn't rest today." She looked up at Mr. Wright. "She needs a place to lie down and rest. Do you have a place where she can rest?"

Marcie drew Beth into her arms, hugging her close. Then she lifted Beth's chin and looked at her so seriously that Beth felt uneasy.

"Beth, Honey, Mommy is very sick, and I need to go to the hospital. Mr. Wright wants you to stay here with him and Mrs. Collins, who gave you the cookies. There are lots of other little girls and boys here and Mr. Wright says you can stay while I am in the hospital. When I get better, I will come back and get you," explained her mother.

Beth's arms circled her mother's neck while her eyes became round with fear. "Mommy, can't I go with you to the hospital? I will be quiet and won't make any noise," pleaded Beth.

Marcie Riley began trying to loosen the clasp of a locket she had always worn around her neck. Taking it off, she quietly placed it around Beth's neck.

"Honey, you can't go with Mommy to the hospital, but I will come back for you. That's why I'm putting my locket on you. You know I would not leave my locket, don't you?"

Beth put her small hand up and touched the locket, which was always clasped around her mother's neck. She looked up at her mommy and smiled a watery smile.

"Will you come back tomorrow, Mommy?" Her mommy bent over, convulsed with coughing. When it subsided, she hugged Beth closely, but said, "No, Honey, not tomorrow but as soon as I can."

Beth stood looking at her mother. "Mommy, I'll be all alone if you don't take me with you. I don't know these people." Big tears were rolling down her cheeks as she looked pleadingly at her mother.

Ethel bent down to Beth's level. "Honey, don't you want your mother to get better? She must have some medicine that only the hospital can give her and there is no place for you to stay at the hospital. Please try to understand."

Mrs. Collins sat down beside Beth and taking her onto her lap said, "Bethy, let's pretend I'm your grandmother and I'll take care of you until your mother gets better. Can we do that?" asked Mrs. Collins and Beth looked up into her kind face and tried to smile.

Nestling into this kind woman's lap, she said, "I've only seen my grandmother once, but I'd like for you to be my grandmother, Mrs. Collins." Then she turned to her mother who was silently crying and trying to keep from coughing.

"Mommy, I want you to be better, so, I'll stay here, and I'll be good, but you come back for me as soon as you're better," said Beth getting down from Mrs. Collins's lap to hug her mother again.

Marcie Riley had another bout of coughing and Ethel hurried to get her some water. When the coughing had eased somewhat, Marcie patted Beth's arm and said, "Thank you, Beth. I want you to remember that I love you very much. I promise that I will come for you as soon as I get better. You go on with Mrs. Collins and I'll call Mr. Wright to check on you."

Then Marcie cuddled Beth in her arms again and hugged her so close that it hurt. Beth wriggled slightly and Marcie kissed her cheek and then released her.

Beth clasped the hand Mrs. Collins put out and together they went toward the door. Just as the door opened to let them pass through, Beth looked back at her mother with tears running down her cheeks.

"You get better soon and Mommy, I'll take

care of your locket. Bye, Mommy."

Hand in hand, Mrs. Collins and Beth went on out the door, and that was the last time Beth Riley ever saw her mother.

Mrs. Collins took Beth to the dormitory which she would share with eight other little girls.

When Mrs. Collins saw her look of terror she said, "Bethy, I'm going to let you stay with me in my room until you get acquainted. Do you want to do that?" she asked.

"Yes, please, Mrs. Collins." Beth gripped the hand that led her back down the hallway to a big room in the front of the building.

As Mrs. Collins began to help Beth unpack her things, Beth started talking about her parents.

"Mommy and Daddy always laughed and played with me. Sometimes they would take me to a little park where there were ducks swimming in a pond. We would have a picnic and then feed the bread scraps to the ducks. Each of them would hold my hand and sometimes swing me as we walked home. We were happy," said Beth as fresh tears ran down her cheeks.

"My daddy told me all about the beautiful green country where he was born. It is called Ireland and my daddy was so happy when he told me about how green everything was at his home. He lived in a big, big house with lots of rooms and he had a dog and horses. He said he dreamed of taking me and mommy to his favorite fishing hole and meeting all his family, especially his sister Agnes. He said she paints beautiful pictures," said Beth as she smiled happily.

Mrs. Collins felt she needed to talk and therefore encouraged her. "You have such good times to remember, Beth. Some of the little girls living here never saw their mommies or their daddies," explained Mrs. Collins.

"I saw my mommy and my daddy, but they put my daddy in a hole and left him there. Daddy didn't go to that mean, mean Jesus," Beth stated this in a resentful voice.

Mrs. Collins gasped in shock and started to explain, but seeing Beth's troubled face, she thought it better to wait before she tried to give any explanation. Instead she asked, "Your mommy and daddy loved each other, didn't they, Bethy?"

"Oh yes, they did. When we went to the park, Mommy always played with Daddy's hair," said Beth with a smile.

"While I fed the ducks, Mommy would sit on the grass and Daddy would lay down with his head in Mommy's lap. Mommy was so happy, and she ran her fingers through Daddy's wavy red hair."

"I'll bet his hair was just like yours. Your Daddy was handsome, wasn't he, Beth?" asked Mrs. Collins.

"My daddy is . . . was the tallest, and most handsomest, man in the world. Mommy told everybody about how handsome he was," enthused Beth said and then lapsed into silence as she sat remembering.

She recalled that sometimes she would go into the living room and her mother and daddy would be talking very seriously. Her mother would be upset because her daddy had asked her to go with him to meet his people in Ireland.

"I want Beth to know her people, Marcie. I know they would love you and her very much," said Jamie, even though he had never gotten a reply to any of his letters.

Beth's father had also begged her mother to agree to go to some hospital in a place called Lewisburg, West Virginia because of her coughing.

In her mind, Beth remembered asking, "Mommy, why don't you want to go? Daddy said it would make you feel better."

Her mother had replied, "They wouldn't let you and your daddy stay with me so I will not go." Beth didn't say anything because she wouldn't want to be anywhere that her daddy couldn't be, but she didn't tell Mrs. Collins that.

Instead, Beth began to tell Mrs. Collins

about her mother's illness. "Mommy's cough got so bad that she took medicine six times a day. She had to lie down all day most of the time. I was always quiet so she could sleep."

Then Beth smiled and plucked at Mrs. Collins' hand. But you know what, when my daddy came home, he called me "his little helper" and tied an apron on me so I could set the table while he cooked our dinner. Daddy always made Mommy feel so much better, but she still couldn't go to the park anymore," finished Beth sadly.

Beth didn't know this for a long time, but later she was told that when her mommy left with Mrs. Collins, Marcie Riley had turned to Mr. Wright with tears in her eyes.

"I'll be back for her as soon as I get better. In the meantime, will you let me know how she is and if she seems to like living here? I couldn't stand it if she was afraid and unhappy. Will you do that Mr. Wright? Also, remember, she is never to be adopted by anyone."

Mr. Wright nodded his head in understanding, but still protested, "Mrs. Riley, I still think you should have an alternative plan just in case you have to stay in the hospital longer than you expect."

Marcie violently shook her head between coughs. "No, Mr. Wright, you don't understand. Beth's father had no people and my people wanted nothing to do with me, except for one aunt who didn't come around much, but I don't know where she is for certain. I once heard she may be in some place in West Virginia."

Mr. Wright, seeing that Marcie was unable to stand much longer, readily agreed and along with Ethel, helped her out to the waiting taxi. Although Ethel Ross called about Beth, Mr. Wright did not talk to Beth's mother again. However, he knew that Mrs. Riley was steadily getting worse and was not surprised when the hospital called to report her death three months later.

# CHAPTER 6

True to her word, Mrs. Collins allowed Beth to stay in the room with her for the first month. On the first day, however, Mrs. Collins introduced Beth to Irene and Peggy, and Beth liked them both. Soon, the three girls became the school's 'Three Musketeers' since they were inseparable.

Irene and Peggy were so excited to have a friend from a big city like Pittsburgh and Beth was just as happy to have her first best friends.

They had lots of games and other things they did in the play area of the dormitory. Without realizing it or intending it to happen, Beth became the leader.

When Beth tried to get Peggy to choose a game Peggy's reply was, "But Beth, you can read and print your name so I think you should pick the games." As expected, Beth spent every waking moment with her two best friends.

One evening, after she had been at the school a month, she went to Mrs. Collins. "Would it be all right if I stayed one night with Irene and Peggy in the dormitory? I think I might like it, but I don't know, and I don't want to hurt you. I like staying with you, but the others are calling me names and saying I'm a baby face. I don't like it when they laugh at me."

Mrs. Collins was relieved since she knew she had to move Beth soon whether she wanted to be moved or not, so she smiled and said, "That's a good idea, Bethy. You try it tonight. I think you'll like being with Irene and Peggy."

The next morning, she hurried to Mrs. Collins' room. "Mrs. Collins, I like being with you and you are good to me, but you are not my mommy. If I move, I'll be just like Irene and Peggy and live in the dorm room with the other girls. Then they won't laugh at me anymore, will they?"

She looked uncertain, but Mrs. Collins smiled and hugged her close. "I think that is a wise choice, Bethy and you can always come to me if you need to. I'll be right here."

She took Beth's hand and said, "Let's go see what Irene and Peggy have to say. Do you think they will like having you in the room with them from now on?" asked Mrs. Collins.

"Oh yes, I know they will because they have been begging me to move anyway," said Beth with a happy smile on her face.

She looked up at Mrs. Collins. "It's so nice to have best friends, isn't it? I've never had best friends before."

The two girls were very excited when they saw Mrs. Collins with all of Beth's clothes.

Peggy met them at the door. "Beth, we can put a bed between mine and Irene's. Then you'll have a friend on each side of you," said Peggy as if bestowing a great treasure and Beth thought it was.

Once the bed was set up and was covered with sheets and a blanket, Beth sat down on the bed and looked around at the other beds in the room and then smiled.

"This will be my home, won't it?" said Beth since in a way it was her home now. This was where Mrs. Collins had brought her on the day her mother left her at Mountain Mission School.

Once Beth was settled in the dormitory and decided that she liked her bed, she was taken to the Preschool section of the school. There were several girls and boys near her own age in the room occupied with various pursuits.

Later, Beth thought back on her first meeting with her new friends. *I didn't think that a thin little blond-headed girl named Irene would become my first best friend,* she thought since she didn't meet Peggy until later.

Beth remembered Mrs. Collins calling for Irene, who came over with a smile and Mrs. Collins told her, "Irene, this is Beth Riley. She has just arrived, and her mother had to go to the hospital, so she needs a best friend. You remember how Peggy helped you when you first came—well I want you to be Bethy's 'Peggy.' I want you to be her friend and a special buddy like Peggy was to you. Okay?"

Irene smiled but stood looking at Beth for

a moment and then shyly picked up her hand and said, “It ain’t so bad. Really, it ain’t. They’ve been good to me. Come on and let’s go play with Peggy. Peggy is my best friend and now you can be my best friend, too.”

Beth smiled and walked away with Irene, still holding her hand. They stopped at a table where a little dark-haired girl with large brown eyes hidden behind glasses with very thick lenses was working on a wooden puzzle.

“Peggy, we have a new best friend. This is Beth Riley. Her mommy is sick and had to go to the hospital. Beth must stay with us until her mommy gets better,” said Irene. Thus, Irene and Peggy became the two best friends that Beth Riley had ever had.

Having best friends was great and it made Beth feel better in the daytime. It did not, however, keep Beth from crying herself to sleep many nights before she became adjusted to the fact that she no longer had a daddy or a mommy to come for her.

That awful Friday afternoon when Mr. Wright called her to his office, a big hole opened in Beth’s heart. She knew it would never be filled again.

Beth had been having a good day in her lessons with the other children and with her new friends. She had adjusted to the fact that her mommy was sick, but she knew her mommy would come back for her. She wasn't like all these other poor children that would be here forever, like Irene and Peggy. It had been two weeks since she had awakened at night and cried, but then that awful Friday changed that.

Mr. Wright was so kind, and Mrs. Collins was there, just like she had been in November when Beth had first arrived. However, neither of them knew an easy way to tell a five-year-old girl, that her mommy had died, without breaking her heart all over again.

On that Friday, not knowing about the trauma of her dad's death, Mr. Wright called Mrs. Collins to bring Beth to his office. Beth came in smiling and laughing with Mrs. Collins clasping her hand warmly. Mr. Wright came around the desk and shook Beth's hand and asked her to be seated as if she were a grown-up lady.

Beth smiled happily and sat in the chair offered. Some of her friends had gotten a summons to Mr. Wright's office and had come back with pretty clothes or letters—maybe she would get something. *Mommy has sent me a letter* thought Beth, with an eager smile.

Mr. Wright pulled up a chair facing Beth and Mrs. Collins. He reached over and picked up both her hands and asked how she liked living with all the other children and Mrs. Collins.

Beth looked thoughtful and then said, "I miss my mommy, but I like it here."

"Good, good!" said Mr. Wright. "We like having you here. Would you mind living here from now on until you finish high school?"

Beth, who was beginning to feel apprehensive, looked at Mr. Wright with very serious eyes, "I like going to school here, but Mommy will be coming to get me soon. See, she gave me her locket to wear," she pulled the locket outside the neck of her blouse and displayed it.

Mr. Wright, who still held one of her hands, squeezed it gently. "No, Honey, your mommy can't come and get you. She has gone to live with Jesus."

The scream that erupted from the small fury who was pounding him in the chest was like a death cry from a wounded animal.

"No, no," screamed Beth. "I hate Jesus—I hate him—hate—hate. I'm going to my mommy," shrieked Beth as she darted for the door.

The gardener, coming to report a shipment, came through the door only to be shoved backward by the enraged five-year-old.

Knocked off balance, old Charlie grabbed Beth as he stumbled and then fell, still clutching the shrieking Beth close to his chest. The wind was knocked out of Charlie and the impact served to subdue and silence Beth.

Mrs. Collins gathered the small shivering body in her arms and crooned softly, "Oh little Bethy, I'm so sorry. I can't be your Mommy, but I'll take care of you. I love you, Bethy . . . we all do."

Looking down, Mrs. Collins knew her words were unheard by the wide-open staring eyes. Beth was in a coma, which they later learned was brought on by the traumatic shock.

Mr. Wright carried Beth to Mrs. Collins' room where she was put to bed while the doctor was called. Dr. Richardson came and checked her over. He closed his bag and stood quietly looking at this beautiful little child, who had now lost both of her parents.

"There's nothing physically wrong with her, but I can't say for sure how soon she will come out of this coma or shock if she ever does." Dr. Richardson walked to the door and then turned.

"You will need to treat her with patience and gentleness. I think she will gradually come out of it. Can you sleep with her and act like a mother to her until she does?"

Mrs. Collins looked at Mr. Wright and at his nod of approval she said, "I will be glad to. She stayed with me for the first month she was here, and she will feel safe with me. Bethy is such a sweet and intelligent child."

A week went by before there was any response, but finally, after prayers on Sunday when the entire school had prayed for Beth, she opened her eyes.

She, however, sat like a wax doll or a robot who couldn't talk. She only sat or lay and stared straight ahead. Another week passed in this manner and Mrs. Collins was so worried. On Sunday morning, a local choir was scheduled to sing at the school auditorium.

Mrs. Collins' room was on the side of the building next to the auditorium, which enabled her to hear what was going on in the auditorium, especially with her windows open. She wanted to hear the singing and didn't think it would bother Beth since she was still not responding even though her eyes were open.

"She acts like a robot. She just stares and does what I tell her, but it isn't normal," reported Mrs. Collins when the doctor made his visit.

# CHAPTER 7

On Sunday morning a month later, Mrs. Collins sat by the window and listened. The choir had sung 'Blessed Assurance' and 'Holy, Holy, Holy,' in sweet clear voices. They began 'Amazing Grace,' and it was very beautiful. Mrs. Collins looked towards Beth who still lay on the bed and tears were running down Beth's cheeks.

Mrs. Collins jumped from her chair, and sat on the bed, before gathering Beth into her arms.

"Hello, Bethy. Have you decided to come back to us?"

Beth threw her arms around Mrs. Collins' neck and cried until she was snubbing. Mrs. Collins remained very quiet while rocking and holding Beth in her motherly arms.

Finally, Beth looked up and said, "That's the song they sang when they put Daddy in that big hole. I guess they are singing it for Mommy, aren't they?"

Mrs. Collins blinked tears from her own eyes as she rubbed Beth's hair, "Yes, Honey, they're singing that for your mommy. It is so pretty. Your mommy would like that, wouldn't she?"

Beth was still for a minute and then said, "Yes, my mommy would like that. Let's just not talk about it anymore. I think I'll get up and go see Irene and Peggy. May I do that Mrs. Collins?"

"Seeing your friends will be good, Honey, but since you've had such a long sleep, you may feel weak. Why don't I get Irene and Peggy to come in here and see you? Maybe, in a few days, when you feel better, you may want to go back to the dorm with them," offered Mrs. Collins.

She saw that Beth liked the idea and so she said, "Let's go in the bathroom and wash your face and hands so you'll be pretty when they come."

Beth slowly climbed out of bed and took Mrs. Collins' hand but was so weak that Mrs. Collins carried her to the bathroom. She sat on the lid of the toilet seat and allowed Mrs. Collins to wash her.

*Now I'm just like Irene and Peggy. They don't have a mommy either. Irene and Peggy have a daddy, but they don't know where they are,* thought Beth, and then decided that, if Irene and Peggy could make it without a mommy, she could too.

"It hurts to not have a mommy and a daddy, doesn't it. Mrs. Collins?" asked Beth as she was carried back to her bed.

"Yes, it does hurt Bethy, and I'm so sorry," replied Mrs. Collins.

"I'm not going to talk about it anymore, and then it won't hurt so much," said Beth, as she was placed back on the bed, to wait for

Irene and Peggy.

"Will you be all right, Bethy, while I get Irene and Peggy?" asked Mrs. Collins and on Beth's nod went quietly out of the room.

So, Bridget Elizabeth (Beth) Riley learned early to accept what could not be changed. From that day forward, she started on her path to becoming a very thoughtful and determined woman. Also, from that day forward Beth was on a path of learning. She learned many things, such as how to make her bed, empty her food tray at meals, dress without help, comb her hair, take her bath without help, and do numerous other chores like helping to wash fruit jars, since her hands were small.

She also was learning to read books and write from her lessons in Preschool. Learning was never a chore for Beth Riley. She was reading far above her grade level by the time she finished the first grade and did almost as well in math, but she wasn't as athletic as either Irene or Peggy.

When she couldn't jump rope or dribble a basketball, she soon got the name 'red-headed klutz' which caused Irene and Peggy many reprimands for fighting since they always defended her.

Having never forgotten that feeling of peace she'd felt when she'd first seen the water wheel down at the gate, she wanted to go and sit by the water wheel, but when she mentioned it to anyone, she was forbidden to go. *When I get a little older, I'll go and just not tell anybody,* she thought but the more she was involved with her friends and her lessons, the less she thought of it.

By the time she was in the third grade, she was such an avid reader that her academic achievements soon became problems. Boredom weighed heavy on her, and she tended to talk to the other students, which disrupted the class.

History was one of her favorite subjects and therefore her heroes or heroines were people like Abraham Lincoln, Thomas Jefferson, Daniel Boone, Amelia Earhart, Joan of Arc, Harriet Tubman, and Susan B. Anthony being her favorites at that time.

Ms. Simmons, a new teacher, called her out for not attending when the class was discussing Black Beauty and Beth said, "I know that story already. I read it last year."

Thinking she was just trying to find some excuse for her behavior, Ms. Simmons said, "Fine, then you tell the class the story."

Beth looked around and saw Jimmy Perkins sniggering since he was always pestering her. She turned red but said, "I will, but I think they'll get more out of it if they read it for themselves."

Ms. Simmons still thought she was stalling

and didn't know the story, so she said, "I'm waiting."

Beth drew in a breath and began. "In this book, the horse is telling the story. We all know that horses can't talk, well not like we talk, but anyway, the horse tells such a sad story about how he has been treated. He is finally bought by a kind man whose daughter loved horses and so Black Beauty became her own special horse.

"Because of that love, the girl gave up her dream of winning a special race because she feared it would hurt the horse. Black Beauty, however, loved the girl so much that he wanted to please her.

"When I read this story, I felt so sad and I thought that Anna Sewell, the author, wanted people to love horses and all living creatures.

"We can learn lots of things from reading and from this book I learned that love has much more power than greed, hate . . . Beth halted and swallowed, before she whispered, "or even fear."

Ms. Simmons and the class sat in stunned amazement, but the bell rang for the next class, and nobody said anything. After school that day, however, Ms. Simmons met with the other teachers in the teacher's lounge and told them what had happened.

Most of the older teachers sat with knowing smiles, but Ms. Jacobs, the math teacher said, "She knows more than my third-grade students in math as well. She helps Peggy and Irene and I think she may be doing their homework."

With encouragement from the other faculty members, Ms. Jacobs, her math teacher, and Ms. Simmons, her English and Reading teacher, went to see Mr. Ratliff, the Principal.

"Mr. Ratliff, we realize that we are here to make an unusual request, but we fear we would be unfair to this student if we did not make it."

Mr. Ratliff put down his pen and looked up at the two women. "What has Jimmy Perkins done this time?"

Both teachers smiled. Ms. Simmons spoke up. "Jimmy is a handful, but we wish to talk about Beth Riley."

"Beth Riley! What's she done?" questioned, Mr. Ratliff, in a surprised voice.

"She hasn't done anything but amaze all of us with her intelligence," said Ms. Jacobs.

"We think Beth should be moved to the fifth grade, for most of the fourth-grade teachers have the same problem when she is in their classes. She's bored and wants to talk during class. When we question her, she already knows the material we are teaching," said Ms. Simmons.

Mr. Ratliff sat turning his pen around and around on his ink blotter, which rested on his desk. "Have you thought about all the social problems this could cause? Beth Riley is much smaller, and two years younger than any of the fifth-grade students, isn't she?"

The two teachers had already talked to the other teachers and Ms. Jacobs spoke up. "We've talked to every one of her teachers and we all know that she is so bored in her third and fourth-grade lessons that she unintentionally gets into trouble or causes disruptions in the classrooms."

"Are you saying she is disrespectful?" asked Mr. Ratliff.

"No, Beth Riley would never be disrespectful. She's nice, kind, and wants to learn, but she disrupts the class by asking questions that the other students would never even think of asking," explained Ms. Simmons.

"Perhaps we could just get her involved in choir and other school functions and she will be all right where she is," said Mr. Ratliff.

"She's already in the choir and in the band and she's reading *Anne of Green Gables*. If you'd sit in on some of her classes, I think you'd see why we are pushing this issue," said Ms. Jacobs.

Mr. Ratliff thought for a moment. "So, this has been discussed with her other teachers and they all think she should be moved? Don't forget that this is an eight-year-old little girl who will be thrust among ten and twelve-year-old students."

Mr. Ratliff sat reading the reports from most of her other teachers and then looked at both women for several minutes. He finally nodded his head and sighed.

"Go ahead, and I hope to heaven all of you are right and it doesn't harm her in other ways."

"We discussed this with several other teachers, and we all have the same concerns as you have, Mr. Ratliff, but we still feel that it is the best thing to do," said Ms. Jacobs.

# CHAPTER 8

Thus, the once third-grade student became a fifth-grade student. Academically, it was the right move, but socially it became very difficult for Beth. She still played with Peggy and Irene since she still shared their space in the dorm, but somehow, it wasn't the same.

It unexpectedly came to a head as the three girls sat working a puzzle. When Beth noticed that Irene and Peggy were mostly talking to each other she rose from her seat and spoke up.

"Peggy, you and Irene act like you don't like me anymore. What have I done?" asked Beth as she waited, hesitantly. The two girls looked quickly at each other and then joined hands.

"You're smarter than we are. Jimmy Perkins tells everybody that. He said you was acting 'too big for your britches,' and you are," said Irene.

"I'm not acting any different. You're just listening to that mean Jimmy Perkins because you like him," said Beth in an angry and upset voice.

Seeing that Beth was upset, Peggy quickly moved to her side. "We do like you, Beth, but you're not free to play with us like before they put you in fifth grade. I know you're smarter than we are, but I wish they hadn't moved you."

"I didn't ask to be moved, Peggy. The teachers went to Mr. Ratliff and asked him to move me. I think Ms. Jacobs found out that I was doing Irene's homework," said Beth.

"I didn't tell her. How did she find out?" asked Irene suspiciously.

"I don't know, Irene. I just heard that she and Ms. Simmons were talking in the hall and Ms. Jacobs said she thought I was doing homework for you and Peggy. I never did sign my name or anything like that, so I don't know why she thought I was," stated Beth.

Peggy shrugged. "Well, you did do our work sometimes and I guess she knows we're not as good in our lessons as you are."

Beth sat back down at the table where the unfinished puzzle still lay. She sat for a moment and then said, "So, other than what Jimmy Perkins said, how am I different?"

"We can't plan nothing. You always have something else you need to do," said Peggy.

Beth dropped her head. "I know. I'm in the choir, in drama class, and in ballet, and I like all of them. I guess you want me to drop out. Is that the difference you're talking about?"

"See, you have got too 'big for your britches' just like Jimmy said," scolded Peggy.

"No, I have not, Peggy. I just like learning new things and I'll bet you'll want to do the same when you get to fifth grade." Beth turned to Irene.

"Irene. do you feel the same way Peggy does?" questioned Beth.

Irene looked at Peggy for a moment and then turned back to Beth. "It's hard, Beth. You see Peggy was the first friend I had when I was brought here and, . . . I can't . . . . not be for her."

Tears pooled in Beth's eyes as she jumped up from the table causing her chair to tilt backward and fall to the floor. "Okay, then. I guess I'll just go." She ran out the door and down the hall.

Mrs. Collins stopped her. "Beth Riley, what's the matter? You know you aren't supposed to run in the halls." She looked down at the tear-drenched face and suddenly stooped and wrapped Beth in her arms.

"Why are you crying, Little Bethy? Who hurt you?" asked Mrs. Collins.

Beth put her arms around Mrs. Collins' waist and stood crying but not aloud. Finally, she looked up into the face of her dearest friend and said, "I just don't fit anywhere. Peggy and Irene don't want to be with me anymore and the fifth graders call me names and don't want to be with me either. Where do I belong Mrs. Collins?"

Mrs. Collins crimped her lips together and mumbled aloud. "I was afraid of this, but they didn't ask me."

Beth stopped crying and stood looking up at Mrs. Collins. "What were you afraid of Mrs. Collins? Did I do something wrong?"

Mrs. Collins grasped her hand and said, "Come on, you and I need to have a talk. Let's go out under our favorite tree."

In the backyard of the girl's dorm, a large oak tree spread its branches to form a canopy of softly fluttering leaves as any tiny waft of wind sprang up. This had been Beth's favorite place to go from the time she first discovered it.

That first time Mrs. Collins found Beth there, she was rolled into a ball of grief. Mrs. Collins bent down beside her and said, "Oh my! You've found a good spot to let your grief spill out, haven't you?"

Beth sat up and turned to look at Mrs. Collins. "What do you mean 'spill' out?"

Mrs. Collins gathered Beth into her arms and sank into the soft earth beneath the tree. She tilted Beth's face up. "I think that sometimes the things that hurt so much get bottled up inside of us and we need to let it 'spill' out and get rid of it."

Beth sat in round-eyed wonder. "I like that. I let all that hurt 'spill' right out and it went right down into the ground. Now I feel better. Thank you, Mrs. Collins. You are smart like my daddy. He told me once that if we try to help somebody else when we are sad that it makes us forget about our own sadness."

Mrs. Collins hugged Beth more snuggly. "Hm-m. I like that, and it is true. Your daddy was very smart."

Beth smiled. "He was handsome, too. Mommy always said Daddy was the handsomest man in the whole world."

That day, Mrs. Collins sat holding her for about ten minutes and then said, "Well, since you've 'spilled' all your grief, can we go back to the playground?"

Beth scrambled to her feet and said, "Yes, but this is a good place to 'spill' grief, isn't it?"

Mrs. Collins got to her feet also and brushed her skirt front and back as she smiled at Beth. "Yes, it is a good place to 'spill' grief. Let's just call it our 'spilling' tree. How about that?"

Beth smiled. "Okay, and let's not tell anyone else. It can be our secret tree." So that became their special place and today Beth needed to 'spill some grief.

Once they were seated, Mrs. Collins put her arm around Beth. "What happened back there with Irene and Peggy? Are they mad at you?" asked Mrs. Collins.

Beth sighed. "Maybe, but I don't really know. They said I was different and didn't spend any time with them."

She didn't say anything for a moment and

then she added, "That's true. I don't play with them as much. I'm so involved with ballet, the band, and the choir that I'm awfully busy."

Beth sat looking at Mrs. Collins with such a sad expression on her face. Just as Mrs. Collins started to speak, Beth spoke.

"You know, Mrs. Collins, I think I just may be different. I don't like to play the games they play anymore, and I didn't know that until today. Or maybe I just hadn't thought about it until today. Am I getting 'too big for my britches' like Jimmy said?"

Mrs. Collins smiled. "That's just Jimmy saying you are smarter than he is. He is bigger than you so if he is talking about size, then he is 'too big for his britches,' too.

Seeing Jimmy with his pants being too short, since they usually were, Beth laughed.

"I think I'll tell Jimmy that he needs to look in the mirror. I'll bet that makes him stop and think," said Beth.

Mrs. Collins smiled. "He probably doesn't know what 'getting too big for your britches' means. I don't know if I've ever heard it explained either."

"I don't really know either, but I think to Peggy it must mean I'm acting mean or something," said Beth thoughtfully.

# CHAPTER 9

They sat silently for a moment, and then Beth said, "You know, Mrs. Collins, I think some people are different. I mean that some people may not look and act like most of the other people around them. It may be their skin color, their size, or like Benny who has a stutter, and this causes people to say they are different and not treat them kindly. Everybody can't be exactly like everybody else, though, can they?" asked Beth giving Mrs. Collins a very serious look.

Mrs. Collins sat listening in 'wide-eyed' wonder. She's never heard anybody, young or old, explain unkindness, jealousy, and even racism in such a true but simple manner.

She smiled. "No, Bethy, everybody is different in some way, but they all have hearts that hurt, bodies that feel physical pain, and they all want to belong. Some are not allowed that privilege though."

Beth smiled. "I don't want to be mean to people, and I don't care if they are different, Mrs. Collins. I don't like to see people hurt.

"I don't know if I've ever acted mean to anyone, so Peggy must mean that my mind is on other things. Do you think that is what she means, Mrs. Collins?"

Mrs. Collins shook her head as if unsure and then looking into Beth's questioning eyes, she asked, "Bethy, do you like it better in the fifth grade?"

Beth sat thinking for a moment. "Yes, I do like it better. I don't know all the lessons, as I did when I was in third grade, and it makes me want to go to class," said Beth.

Mrs. Collins put her arms around Beth. "I think you are in a different place than Irene and Peggy right now. But it doesn't mean that you don't like them anymore, does it?"

"No, I really like Peggy and Irene and I still want them for my friends. I think it is just different now, for me and for them since I don't like to play some of their games anymore. So, like I said, I don't fit in anywhere now," explained Beth.

"You don't really fit in with the fifth graders either, do you?" asked Mrs. Collins.

Beth looked ready to cry, but she swallowed and looked at Mrs. Collins. "No, they call me 'brains' and 'teacher's pet' and other stuff. I don't think some of them like me. Some of them don't even talk to me, but Benny Schaffer does, and they laugh at him. He stutters and I feel sorry for him, but he is intelligent."

"I guess he understands how you feel, Beth. Benny is a good boy and will be a good friend, I think," said Mrs. Collins.

She realized that Benny was also a misfit. He stuttered and she knew the other students made fun of his stutter, so Mrs. Collins smiled and nodded her head.

"Maybe this is a time to do something for somebody else since your daddy said it would make you feel better. If you are good to Benny and he is good to you, then both of you will be happier and won't feel so out of place," said Mrs. Collins.

Beth smiled. "That's right! I don't laugh at him because he stutters when he reads, but the others do, and that makes him unhappy. He told me he didn't like to go to school here, but if I were his friend, he may like it better. Do you think that will help?" asked Beth.

Mrs. Collins rose to her feet. "Yes, Bethy, I think it will. The fifth grade won't be as hard for you or Benny."

Beth laughed. "That will make learning even easier if I have a friend. Thanks, Mrs. Collins.

Mrs. Collins walked away wondering if she had helped Beth, or Beth had solved her own problem. *That child is something special,* she thought as she went back to the dorm.

The teachers didn't know it then, but until Beth entered his world, Benny was unhappy and often thought of running away from the school. Beth Riley changed all that.

The first day she came to the class, she was seated at a desk just across from Benny.

She looked around and all the other students were so much bigger and older, and they were all glaring at her except the boy across from her.

Benny didn't glare at her, but he did turn to look at her and she smiled. From that day forward, Benny Schaffer became Beth's champion and often had arguments with the other students because of his support for her.

That was when Irene and Peggy found that their triumvirate with Beth was often invaded by Benny. He couldn't come to their dorm, but their talks at lunchtime were invaded by Benny and he became their enemy.

They also discovered that Beth, as a fifth grader, could no longer eat at the third grader's table with Irene and Peggy. Grades one, two, and three ate before the fourth, fifth, and sixth-grade students.

Each section of children had to clean the dishes used for each meal when they finished. The first and second graders did not have to do as much, but they were being trained as they followed the orders of the cooks and each year had to do a little more.

The fifth-grade students rotated with the fourth and sixth-grade students in doing a complete clean-up. They raked out all the scraps into the pails set at each end of the tables, cleaned all the pots, pans, silverware, and dishes, shook out the table linens or put them into the laundry hampers to be washed, and then swept the entire dining room and kitchen.

Beth wasn't very big, but she did everything the other children did while standing on a stool to wash the dishes. She loved doing all this except putting scraps into the pig's bucket. She closed her eyes as she raked since looking into the pail made her feel sick to her stomach.

Benny, who now, always ate beside Beth, saw her revulsion in doing this task and so he said, "Beth, I'll du-dump the sc-scraps and hu-hand you the pl-ates and you pu-put em into the tro-trolley."

Beth smiled in appreciation. "If we hurry, we'll be done before the bell rings, and we can play a while. That will be great, but will it get you into trouble? I don't like it when Cook yells."

Benny grinned. "I-I don't ca-care. She can ye-yell her old ha-head off."

That was their routine after that, and they did finish before the others since they only did one row of tables, but only the side where they were seated. Two other students did the other side. It also became their routine of playing together and doing chores together and Beth felt like she had a brother.

Beth spent time with Benny during the

day when they were in the same classes, but she still lived and slept in the dorm with Peggy and Irene. Even after they had their argument, they were still friends, but Beth was no longer considered 'best friend' or, at least, not to Peggy.

After the move, Beth realized fifth and sixth-grade students were not allowed to visit or play with third-grade students. Benny soon found that there were no exceptions when he tried to see Beth at other times except those designated.

So, during the day and during church services on Sundays, Beth was Benny's pal or friend. The rest of the time, until Irene and Peggy became fifth-grade students, Beth spent her meager play time and evenings exclusively with them.

It became very difficult for the girls to be together since Beth was in most of the academic contests and functions there at the school and she was also in the school choir. These kinds of activities kept her away from the activities of the lower-grade students. So, for the next couple of years, the girls were not as close as they had been earlier, and Beth knew they would never regain that closeness.

This caused Benny to be with her more and she grew to like and respect him. They did not have as much time together as they had at first because Beth was in lots of academic things at school and Benny was involved in sports, but they still sat together at their meals.

However, with the encouragement of Beth, Irene and Peggy joined the choir and soon they became the singing trio. Their voices could be heard anytime they were together. And often in unusual places; like the halls of the education building.

Even though everyone enjoyed their singing, they had to stop except when outside or in their music classes.

So, for the two years before Peggy and Irene were promoted to the fifth grade, they'd had a very erratic pattern of friendship, but now they were again together, and life was much easier for Beth.

That comradery only lasted for one year. At the end of that year, Beth became a seventh grader. She was also chosen to become a part of the performing choir, and she traveled with the choir for their performances.

Also, Benny had hit a growth plateau, and now was a star basketball player, and was the tallest player on the team. Somewhere along the way, Benny also lost his stutter which pleased Beth very much.

"Benny, you don't stutter anymore. What happened?" asked Beth as they ate lunch.

"I don't know, Beth. It still happens

sometimes, but not very often. I'm glad though and nobody picks on me now since I'm so tall," said Benny with a broad smile.

So, both Beth and Benny had grown, learned, and were still the very best of friends.

Beth had also grown into a very attractive girl, with youthful curves in the right places, twinkling brown eyes, and a mass of shiny auburn hair even if she was still small in stature. The label of being 'too big for her britches' was still sometimes attached to Beth, but not by her male classmates. The taunt didn't have much effect on her now, for something else took precedence in her life.

# CHAPTER 10

Beth, being in the eighth grade when Irene and Peggy became fifth-grade students, found herself helping her two friends again, but not as often as they wished.

They, however, were raised in Mountain Mission School and did not need the help that a new girl would need.

That is what happened though, and this event changed the life of Beth Riley, forever. It also put another hindrance to the close friendship between the three girls, which was never fully regained.

This change happened so unexpectedly that Beth later felt that it was destined by a higher power. At that time, though, she still did not have a close relationship with Jesus.

Beth now knew the story about Jesus and accepted it. Gradually she realized that sickness and accidents happened to everybody, but Jesus didn't cause them. *Jesus is here to help us and give comfort when hurtful things happen to us,* she thought as she gave a contented sigh.

In one of their sessions under their 'spilling' tree, Beth said, "Mrs. Collins, I see the real Jesus now. I think that when bad things happen to us, Jesus is always there to help and give us comfort and He promised to take us to heaven when we die."

Beth smiled as she looked at Mrs. Collins

and said, "I believe that Jesus sent me here so I could have you, the only grandmother I will ever know."

Mrs. Collins hugged Beth closely and slow, silent tears crept down her cheeks as she whispered, "Yes, Dear, I feel the same way. I don't have any grandchildren and Jesus sent you to me so that you could be my only granddaughter."

Beth smiled and hugged Mrs. Collins and then suddenly said, "He makes good things happen, like bringing me to Mountain Mission School so that you and I could be together and when we die Jesus will call us home to Heaven where we will always be with each other, won't we?"

Mrs. Collins wiped her face and eyes and rose to her feet and smiled as she said, "Yes, Honey, that's why we love Jesus so much. He really does take care of His children, even when they get old like I am."

Now Beth was sorry that she had once thought she hated Jesus. Mrs. Collins told her to not blame herself, since nobody had told her about Jesus back then. From the events that happened later in her life at Mountain Mission School, she had no doubt that Jesus was in control of her life.

The day that this was made clear to Beth was a normal day, except it was the day that

Mrs. Collins came to see her. When Mrs. Collins came into the lunchroom to find her, Beth was startled since this was very unusual.

Beth felt a tap on her shoulder and turned to find Mrs. Collins. Before Beth had time to ask anything, Mrs. Collins whispered, "Beth, I know you remember how you felt when you first came here, and I feel you can be of help. Are you willing to help another little girl?"

Beth gave Mrs. Collins a puzzled look as she rose from the table. "What little girl? Is she new? Where is she?"

Mrs. Collins motioned for Beth to follow her. When they were in the hall where they couldn't be heard, Mrs. Collins said, "Beth, a little girl, Marlo Stevens, has just arrived. She's had a terrible life and she is scared out of her wits right now. I felt that you were the only person in the entire school that she could probably relate to since her mother went to the hospital, as your mother did."

Beth's face turned pale as a memory flashed before her eyes, and without any hesitation she said, "Yes, I'll do whatever I can. When can I see her?"

Mrs. Collins explained that they had to tell all of Beth's teachers about what they planned to do. This was after she told Beth about the horrible shape that Marlo was in. "She won't be easy to work with, Beth. She's afraid of everybody and she's grief-stricken over her mother."

"Mrs. Collins, I don't know whether I can help her or not. Do you think I can?" questioned Beth with a worried frown.

"I don't know for sure, but Mr. Wright and I talked it over and we feel certain that she would trust someone her own age quicker than she would trust an adult," said Mrs. Collins.

So, after clearing it with Beth's teachers, the rest of that day and every day thereafter, Beth Riley became a mentor, sister, friend, and mother to Marlo Stevens.

Beth followed Mrs. Collins to Mr. Wright's office and when she stepped through the door, she struggled to keep from fainting as the big violet eyes of the little 'bag of bones' with a black and blue face, and long black curling hair looked up at her.

Grasping Mrs. Collins' arm, Beth steadied herself and then walked slowly to the chair placed beside this pitiful apparition. Beth quietly sat down, and Mrs. Collins took a chair on the other side of Marlo Stevens.

"Marlo, this is Beth Riley. She was brought here by her mother, too, because her mother also had to go on to the hospital. Beth is in school here, and she wants to be your friend. How do you feel about that?" asked Mrs. Collins.

The small, bruised face with its startling

violet eyes, turned to gaze warily at Beth. Although Beth fought the tears which sprang up in her eyes, she tried to smile, and without even thinking she found herself praying, *Lord, please forgive me. When I came here, I thought that nobody ever suffered the way I was, but this must be worse,* thought Beth as she sat trying to regain control.

"I'd like to be your friend," said Beth and smiled through her tears.

Marlo's swollen lips and jaw jerked in her effort to smile, but she jerkily mumbled, "Yes, I …" she didn't get any farther because a loud wail rose from those trembling lips as she put out a trembling hand.

Beth didn't take her hand, but instead, she folded Marlo in her arms. "Oh, Honey, I'm so sorry for your suffering. Please let me be your friend. I'll take care of you, and you won't have to hurt anymore."

Marlo's tortured body seemed to melt into Beth's embrace as she sobbed softly. Beth held her until her sobs gradually stopped and both Ms. Collins and Beth were astonished to realize that Marlo had gone to sleep.

Beth and Mrs. Collins let out hopeful sighs and turned to Mr. Wright, who had stepped in from another room. "Mr. Wright, I think she will trust Beth."

Mr. Wright looked at Beth. "Do you feel

the same way?"

Beth nodded and he continued. "You can put a bed beside you in the dorm . . ." but Beth stopped him.

"I think we need to have a room by ourselves, like Mrs. Collins and I did when I first came here. I . . . I don't think she will talk if there is anyone else to hear her. Could we have a room until she gets better and is calmer than she is now?" asked Beth cautiously looking for approval.

Mrs. Collins looked at Mr. Wright and nodded and then he said, "This won't be easy for you, Beth. Do you think you can handle it with all the other things you do?"

Beth looked down at the battered body nestled against her and nodded as she looked steadily at Mr. Wright. "I may need some help, but I want to try. She needs me," whispered Beth from trembling lips.

Mr. Wright hesitated for a moment and then said, "We can try this for a month to six weeks, but if we see it isn't working or if you feel it isn't, then we'll have to try something else. What do you think, Mrs. Collins?"

Mrs. Collins looked at Beth and saw the determined gleam in her eyes. "I think it will work, but I'd like to be near them, just in case it becomes too much for Beth. What about that room across the hall from me? Right now, it's used for storage, but it has a separate bathroom from the dorm bathroom. I think we can find enough beds and things to fix it."

"How long will it take to get it ready? She may not sleep very long, and I don't want her screaming again. It's hard to see that much agony," said Mr. Wright and then as if realizing that Beth would be with it for a long time, he grimaced.

He turned to Mrs. Collins. "Are we asking one of our students to take on this ordeal just to solve our own problem?"

Mrs. Collins looked startled, but before she could say anything Beth said, "I agreed to try and if it becomes too much, I'll tell Mrs. Collins. I just feel she needs me, and this is what I need to do."

## CHAPTER 11

Mr. Scales, from maintenance, came in when Mr. Wright paged him and was given instructions to fix the room up with speed since Beth couldn't sit holding her sleeping bundle for hours.

Beth sat thinking about what could have happened to this pretty, little girl. *Who beat her? Was it her mother, her father, or someone else?* Soon, however, her arms began to ache, and she felt the need to use the bathroom.

She was just ready to try to lay Marlo down on the seat and slip away when Benny, who was a student helper for Mr. Scales, burst through the door.

"Where's Mr. Wright? Mr. Scales wants..." He didn't get any further but jumped back as a wild scream broke forth from the now awake, battered wraith as she broke free from Beth's embrace.

The scream had also startled Beth and caused her to loosen her hold on Marlo. They both fell to the floor, but Beth bore the brunt of the fall. She landed on the floor with Marlo atop her with arms and legs flailing in all directions. Beth was hit in the nose and in one eye, but she did not let go of Marlo.

She struggled and with help from Mrs. Collins, Beth finally got untangled from Marlo and lurched to her feet, but blood was dripping from her nose. She grabbed the towel someone produced and turned her attention to Marlo.

"Marlo. Stop that screaming. Nobody is trying to hurt you. That boy lives here and helps Mr. Scales when he isn't in class. He is helping get a room ready for me and you."

Marlo looked up at Beth, who stood holding a towel under her nose, and stopped screaming, but she looked puzzled.

Beth was having trouble seeing, but she knelt on the floor in front of Marlo. "I can't help you unless you try to help me. You've given me a bloody nose and I don't know what you've done to my eye. Now, pull yourself together and stop screaming."

Beth knew she was talking sternly, but she was hurt, and angry, and her nose was still bleeding. She looked around and Mrs. Collins handed her a wet towel.

"Here, Beth, pinch your nose together with your thumb and finger so it will stop bleeding," said Mrs. Collins as she wiped the blood from Beth's face.

"I can't see very well. I think she poked her finger in my eye, too" said Beth still on her knees beside Marlo.

Marlo reached out with a trembling hand. "I'm sorry. I..." She didn't get to finish for Beth raised to her feet and said, "I'm sorry, too, but I didn't black your eye or bloody your nose."

The other people in the room seemed to be caught up in a tableau vivant until Beth delivered this scold. Then Benny relaxed and unclenched his fists which he had prepared to wade in and help Beth, and Mrs. Collins reached out her hand.

"Here, Beth, let me see if the bleeding has stopped." Beth released the pinch on her nose and turned to Mrs. Collins.

Mrs. Collins smiled. "Well, the screaming and the bleeding have both stopped, but I think you've paid a price for it."

Beth turned back to look at Marlo, who lay stunned. Not knowing whether she was to be knocked into the wall by some of these people, she lay staring at Beth.

Beth looked at Mrs. Collins. "Do you think that you and I can get her to the dorm? I'm afraid to ask anyone else. I just can't stand anymore screaming."

Mrs. Collins smiled grimly. "I'll help, but I don't know if we can take her anywhere unless she is willing."

Beth turned to Marlo. "Marlo, I know you are weak, scared, and worried, but we need to get to our room so you can eat and rest. Will you go with us and not scream all the way?"

Marlo sat up straighter and gave Beth and then Mrs. Collins a wary look. She must have realized that Beth was safe since she hadn't retaliated when she got a bloody nose and a black eye, so she nodded and then mumbled. "Yeah, I'll go."

Beth looked at her for a moment and then asked, "Do you feel able to walk?"

When Marlo nodded, Beth turned to Mrs. Collins. "She needs to be settled so let's give it a try."

So, twenty minutes later, Marlo was lying on a bed in a small room connected to the dorm by a narrow hallway. Both Mrs. Collins and Beth were tired, and Marlo was completely exhausted. She was paler than she had been earlier, and Beth shook her head as she turned toward the door.

"I'm going to the kitchen to see" . . . she was stopped by Marlo's hand reaching out to catch her dress. Beth turned back and said, "I'll be back. You need something to eat."

Marlo had tears in her eyes. "Don't leave me," she whispered, and Mrs. Collins rose from her chair by the door.

"You stay, Beth. I'll get the food. She feels safer with you, I guess," said Mrs. Collins and went through the door.

Beth sat down on the bed beside Marlo. "Marlo, you've been through a bad time, but you will be safe here. I've been here since I was four years old, and nobody has hurt me or treated me badly. It is hard to accept that this is your home, but after you've been here a while, you will like it."

Beth stopped talking as Mrs. Collins came through the door bearing a plate of food.

"Oh good! Marlo, sit up and eat. Then you can go to sleep," said Beth as she looked at Marlo, who was almost asleep.

Seeing that Marlo was having trouble sitting up, Beth pulled her into a sitting position so she could put the plate on her lap. However, she quickly saw that Marlo was too weak to hold her plate in that manner, so, she looked up at Mrs. Collins, who still held the plate.

There was a small table under the one window in the room and Beth released her hold on Marlo, who immediately slumped back onto the bed.

"We'll have to feed her, I guess," said Beth as she stepped to the table. She took the lamp from the table and placed it on a dresser before turning to Mrs. Collins.

"Let's try to get her to sit up, and feed herself if she can. I don't want to start something to make her dependent on others," said Beth, and Mrs. Collins smiled.

"I don't think there's another student in this school who would have thought about that, Beth. Knowing your thirst for independence, though, I can see it coming from you," said Mrs. Collins as Beth put the table in place beside the bed.

Beth ended up feeding Marlo that time, but Marlo quickly became strong enough to take care of her bathing and her meals and was again in school.

For the first month, Beth got little sleep. Marlo would not go to her classes unless Beth took her, so she had to walk Marlo to all her classes and then hurry to her own. She had to be there to take her to her other classes as well, which was taking its toll on Beth.

They hadn't heard anything from Marlo's mother at that time, and Beth hoped she was getting better. Her hopes were dashed that same evening. Mr. Wright called Marlo and Beth to the office and Beth dreaded Marlo's reaction to whatever Mr. Wright had to say.

Mr. Wright met them at the door and offered them a seat. Beth saw that Mr. Wright was hesitant about telling Marlo anything and her heart sank. She once again relived the shock and anguish she had experienced when the same thing had happened to her.

The two girls sat quietly waiting until Mr. Wright said, "Marlo, do you remember what a shape your mother was in when the police found the both of you?"

Marlo's violet eyes blared in wild panic as she asked, "Did he get to her again? I guess he killed her, didn't he?"

Both Beth and Mr. Wright were stunned for a moment, and then Mr. Wright said, "No, Marlo, he is still in prison, but I guess he did kill her. The damage he did the day you were both found was so bad that the doctors couldn't fix it."

Beth stiffened in her seat expecting another wild screaming fit, but it never came. Marlo sat with tears streaming down her face, but not making a sound.

The room was so eerily quiet like it gets before a storm, and then Marlo said, "Mommy told me he was trying to kill us both, but she wasn't going to let him kill me, and she didn't." Nobody said anything and then Marlo continued, "My Mommy really loved me, and I'm glad he don't know he killed her. I'd like to kill him."

# CHAPTER 12

Even though Beth knew that killing somebody was wrong, she understood Marlo's thoughts. "Mrs. Collins says, 'Everything that goes around comes around.'" And when Marlo looked at her like she was crazy, Beth explained.

"She means that if we do wrong, we will get the same treatment sometime in our lives, so perhaps your father will receive the same abuse from somebody," said Beth solemnly.

"I shore hope he does, and I'd like to be the one to do it," said Marlo before dropping her head into her lap and crying, but she didn't scream.

So, feeling responsible for Marlo was good for Beth and Marlo was like a 'work in progress.' She had many little habits that disturbed Beth, but still, everyone could see the improvement in her.

However, as time passed, Beth had grown to love Marlo as if she was her own child. *I know we are the same age, but Marlo is such a child,* thought Beth as she continually tried to shape and mold Marlo into a woman who could survive on her own.

Later, Mr. Wright told Mrs. Collins that he was certainly relieved, and he felt certain that Beth was also. "Beth has accomplished a lot with that girl, hasn't she?"

Mrs. Collins smiled. "She certainly has, but

it is wearing her out."

Each month, Beth could see a change in Marlo, but she had some traits that Beth did not know how to handle. She told everything she knew, and she didn't care to whom she told it.

During this troubling time, an unexpected change in Beth's favor occurred which eased her worries to a small degree and later she was very thankful. Beth had not received a call to come to the office since her mother died and when Mr. Wright sent for her and Mrs. Collins she was filled with fear. Mrs. Collins said, "Honey, he didn't sound sad or worried so I believe it may be something good."

Mr. Wright welcomed them with a big smile on his face, "Miss Beth Riley, you have come into some money. The company that your father worked for has set up a trust for you until you are twenty-one years old. You will get a certain amount each month to spend on your needs, such as clothing, and other small items, but the main amount is being invested for you. So, by the time you are twenty-one years old, there should be a sizeable amount waiting for you."

Beth didn't know what to say, since she was only four years old when her father was killed. "When did they do this?" asked Beth." It has been eleven years since his death. Did they just now set it up?"

"I understand that they set it up right after your father died, but they did not know where you were until recently," said Mr. Wright.

At that moment, Beth was pleased but later she thought *I would rather have had my daddy than have any money at all.*

Before they left Mr. Wright's office, Beth was told to not mention this to anyone else.

Mrs. Collins, said, "Beth, none of the other students have anything like this. Sometimes, children get jealous if another child has more than they have, so let's just keep this to ourselves."

Mr. Wright smiled. "Mrs. Collins will take care of your money here and nobody else needs to know anything about it. Do you think that's a good idea?"

Beth stood thinking for a moment and then said, "Yes Sir, I do think it is a good idea. Irene and Peggy don't have anything like that and if they knew, they may not like me. They are my first 'best friends' and I don't want to lose their friendship."

So, Beth knew she was different, but she also knew that it had to be a secret between Mrs. Collins, Mr. Wright, and herself. Beth forgot all about the money, except occasionally when Mrs. Collins would sneak in a bunny rabbit, a nightgown, a dress, or shoes, supposedly from one of the shipments that came to the store, but they both knew that those things were new.

Thus, Beth's life was just the same as every child at Mountain Mission School and she was glad to have it that way. In the following years, she learned to love the school and most of the teachers. She still heard snide remarks made about her since she was such a good student, but Benny Schaffer was a true friend who was always on her side.

The year that Beth became a senior and Marlo a junior, the struggles began to show in Beth. She was worn thin. Her clothes were now much too large for her, her face was thin as well as her hair, and she had completely lost her appetite.

Finally, Mrs. Collins stopped Beth as she was on her way to choir practice. "Beth, we are going to move Marlo into the dormitory with the other girls, and you are going to see a doctor."

Beth started to protest, but Mrs. Collins said, "Mr. Wright and all the teachers are behind me on this. You may keep the room, you've earned it anyway, but Mr. Wright told me to call and get you an appointment at the hospital."

"Why? I'm not sick. I'm just tired," argued Beth. However, Mrs. Collins nodded with a determined look in her eye and said, "You have an appointment for next Tuesday morning at 10 am with Dr. Berry there at the hospital."

Beth was still a student and knew she had to obey so she nodded and walked on to choir practice. On the way, she realized that she hadn't felt well and happy for several months. Also, her clothes no longer fit, and she knew she couldn't go out and buy all new clothes. That would certainly raise suspicions, but she did plan to ask Mrs. Collins about finding some dresses in her size at the clothing store. *Going to the doctor may be a good thing even if it is forced on me,* she thought.

*I'll always protect Marlo, but she needs to learn some independence and I need a break,* she thought as she entered the music building.

She stopped by the bathroom before going to choir and looked into the mirror over the bathroom sink and was suddenly shocked at the person looking back at her.

Beth's once shining auburn curls, were dull and hung limply down her back. Her sparkling brown eyes didn't seem to gleam, much less sparkle. *What has happened to me,* she thought as she pushed her hands through her hair.

She mumbled aloud. "I'm sixteen years old and I look thirty. How come I haven't noticed?" Then she thought about her doctor's appointment.

*Everyone else has noticed, but I've been so bent on helping Marlo that I've completely forgotten about Beth Riley,* she thought as she dried her hands and left the bathroom.

# CHAPTER 13

Beth liked Dr. Berry, who was new to the area, and he did a thorough examination. "Ms. Riley, I think you are just worn out mentally, physically, and emotionally and you need to get away from whatever has done this to you for a while. Is it possible for you to take a vacation?"

"No, Sir, but I graduate in May and perhaps I may be able to work out something then," said Beth since she really wanted to leave.

"Well, I'm going to give you a tonic and I will call Mr. Wright and tell him that you need fewer duties for a while," said the doctor as he wrote out the prescription.

When she returned to the school Mr. Wright called her into the office. "Beth, the choir is going on tour to Philadelphia, and you are to go with them," said Mr. Wright.

Beth hesitated. "Mr. Wright, I don't know if Marlo's ready for a move like that. She wants to know I'm near all the time. What if she has a relapse?"

"You will only be gone for five days, and this is a good opportunity for you, Marlo, and everyone else to observe how she will do," said Mr. Wright.

Beth went and had a wonderful time since she called back and found that Marlo was fine. She came back looking and acting more like her old, cheerful, optimistic self.

She was very happy when Marlo met her with a smile on her face and gushing about how glad she was to have Beth back where she had access to her. Beth felt like Marlo had, at last, conquered her fears, and now she could rest easier if she couldn't be with Marlo every day.

During the years that she had spent in Mountain Mission School, Beth had grown, but she still was not large. However, as she became a teenager, she developed delightful curves that attracted a lot of attention. Her sparkling brown eyes and long wavy auburn hair, as well as her dimpled smile, finished off the package and she was admired and liked by students and teachers. From her early days, her intellect had been noticed by her teachers and now Beth found herself ready to graduate at a much earlier age than most.

Beth had been pretty, as a child, and she had grown into a beautiful young woman. When Marlo appeared on the scene, however, she took Beth's place as the prettiest girl in the school.

Marlo Stevens was not only the prettiest girl in school, but she also became a daily joy in Beth's life. Until Marlo arrived, Beth had never been concerned about her own looks except for cleanliness, which was a must. She had always focused on her studies and shut everything else out.

However, wanting to be a good example for Marlo, she took more interest in clothing and in presenting a nice image to the public. She had a good 'eye' for stylish apparel, and she encouraged Marlo to do the same. In Marlo, Beth found someone who needed her, someone who loved her, and someone who was willing to listen and accept Beth's decisions.

With this kind of bond, Beth made no decisions about anything without thinking of Marlo. Therefore, when the attention from Mr. Schermets, the science teacher, became more bothersome and lately a reason for fear, Beth made up her mind to leave Mountain Mission School.

*Marlo doesn't like school, so there must be a way that we can slip away together and get completely away before we are missed,* thought Beth as she went about her job as an aide to the science department, and that meant Mr. Schermets.

That same evening, while in the lunchroom, Beth saw what she hoped could be her escape. Jerry Curtis, the food distribution truck driver, came through the door just as she rose to leave. She saw him and stopped. She knew Jerry liked her since he always made it a point to stop and speak to her if they met.

With a big smile she said, "Jerry, I didn't know this was your day to deliver. Is this the only school where you make deliveries?"

Beth had stopped right in front of him. "Were you looking for someone in charge?"

Jerry turned red. "No, I was just going to see if I could get a cup of coffee from the kitchen before I head on out."

"Where do you go from here? I mean, do you make long-distance trips? You do look tired," said Beth as she studied him.

Jerry grinned. "I've been on the road since seven o'clock this morning. I had to go to Pikeville to get a load, and now I only need to go to Iaeger and Welch. That ain't bad, but when I'm scheduled to go all the way to Huntington, West Virginia, that's a two-day trip."

Beth's eyes widened as she realized what this could mean. "How often do you have to do that?" she asked and then continued. "It must be awfully lonely driving all that way by yourself."

"You da . . uh dern right it is. I hate that trip, but it's part of the job."

"Do you have to do that every week?" asked Beth giving him a pitying look.

"No, thank the good Lord, I only need to go there once each month. I always go on the first Thursday of every month. That way I can get there and back before the weekend. The company wants their trucks left in their garage unless they're on some trip.," said Jerry with a smile of pleasure on his face.

This was the first time he'd had a conversation with Beth, and he'd been trying to see her at every opportunity.

Beth stepped in a little closer and almost whispered as she asked, "Jerry, can you keep a secret?"

Jerry's eyes widened, and his face turned redder than usual since he was near Beth. "I sure can. Whatever you tell me in secret will stay a secret."

Jerry smiled and said, "I know your name is Beth so is it all right if I call you that?"

Beth smiled. "Yes, Jerry, you may call me Beth since I really do need your help. Oh, here, take this coffee. I can get me another cup and I haven't drunk from it yet."

"Sure, I'll help you with whatever it is," he quickly offered again.

"Would you let me go with you on your next trip to Huntington? I need to get away, but I don't want anyone to know I'm going. I'm not in any trouble, but there are things I can't tell you right now." Beth stopped and looked around.

Fearing that someone would see her and get suspicious, she stepped back a little. "I'll be working in the clothing store next Saturday. Could you maybe come by there about ten o'clock? Then we can make some plans," said Beth as she cautiously looked toward the kitchen door.

"Sure, I usually come into Grundy on Saturdays anyway. I'll be there," said Jerry with a broad smile.

"Great, but don't tell anybody . . . I mean, nobody, not even your mother," said Beth as she moved slightly away.

"I hear you, Beth, and 'mums' the word. I promise," said a jubilant Jerry Curtis as he turned and walked on toward the door without looking back.

Beth calmly made her way to the kitchen, where she had intended to go anyway. Deborah Harley was peeling potatoes at the sink when Beth entered, and she turned in surprise.

"I thought you came in for coffee a few minutes ago. Did you spill it? There may be a little more in the pot."

Beth smiled. "I was just in here, but I met that delivery man who was headed this way for coffee and gave mine to him. Those truck drivers have such a tight schedule that they don't get many breaks."

Deborah laughed. "I'll be happy when I get old enough to leave here. Maybe Jerry's like me and took any job he could get. I know I will. I'll need to work."

Beth looked concerned. "Is someone being unkind to you, Debbie? You can tell me. I'll never mention your name to anybody."

Deborah shook her head. “No, I’m treated just like everyone else, but we all know this isn’t home. I mean, it isn’t like we’ll want to come back here when we leave, or at least I won’t. I dream about a home like the one I had before that slate fall killed my father. Mom just didn’t know how to take care of six children, and besides, I think she already had tuberculosis.”

Both girls stood quietly for a moment and Beth patted Deborah’s shoulder before saying. “I guess we all have a story, don’t we? Some are worse than others, but we only grieve over our own, most of the time. I’m truly thankful for the education the school has provided, and I’d like to leave too, but I can’t leave until Marlo graduates. She’s all I have.”

Deborah looked stunned. “Is Marlo your sister? You two look nothing alike.”

Beth smiled. “No. We’re not related, but I’ve sort of adopted her and she thinks she can’t survive if I’m not around. So, I’m her sister, mother, or whatever she needs at the time, I guess.

# CHAPTER 14

During the days and nights of trying to calm Marlo's fears when she first arrived, Beth learned Marlo's story. Listening to this beautiful little girl's heart-wrenching story made Beth realize that she had much to be thankful for since her father had been so kind and good.

Marlo, along with her mother had escaped from a brutal beating and were picked up by the police. Marlo's mother was near death when they were found, and she begged the police to take Marlo to Mountain Mission School.

"Go, arrest Jerry Stevens. He has almost killed me, but I wouldn't let him kill my baby. He did beat her, though."

Mrs. Stevens stopped and dropped her head, coughing and gagging as blood filled her mouth and spurted out when she coughed. She moaned pitifully but still moaning, she looked at the policeman. "Please, please arrest him and take my baby to Mountain Mission School."

Since they were found on the road to Poplar Creek, the police stopped at the hospital first. All while this was happening Marlo had clung to her mother's hand and had not spoken or looked up.

The police knew Marlo was also in a bad way, but she was still on her feet and could walk. They felt that Mrs. Stevens wouldn't last long and so all attention was centered on her until they had Mrs. Stevens on a gurney,

That's when the trouble started. They could not get Marlo to let go of her mother's hand. When they tried to talk to her, she acted as if she didn't hear anything. She stood staring and clinging to the hand with all the strength in her small body.

When the doctor forced her fingers from her mother's hand a scream, like the cry of a 'wild banshee,' erupted from her swollen lips, before she whispered "Mommy, Mommy."

She went limp, but the doctor caught her before she hit the ground and she was put on the gurney beside her mother and taken into the emergency room at Buchanan General Hospital.

When she'd told the entire story, Marlo was drained of all emotion, and Beth was filled with sorrow. *I'll never let anyone hurt her again,* thought Beth as she hugged Marlo and told her to try not to think about it anymore.

"Your mother will never be beaten up again and we know your father is in prison, so you are safe. You and I will stay together, and I'll always be your friend, Marlo," promised Beth.

Marlo smiled drowsily. "I know you will, Beth. Thank you." Then, as if on demand, she closed her eyes and slept.

Beth didn't go to sleep though. She spent another hour thinking of how she could leave

Mountain Mission School and take Marlo with her. *Marlo is so pretty she will probably be Mr. Schermets next target, especially if I'm not around,* thought Beth and became more determined to get away.

She knew she could ride with Jerry Curtis, but she had no idea where she wanted to go. *I could go with him to Huntington, but I need to make sure I can survive once I get there,* she thought drowsily but then focused on the other problem.

*I can't stand much more of Mr. Schermet's pats, smiles, and innuendos.* She shivered. *He makes me feel like my skin is crawling,* she thought in revulsion. Finally, she turned over again and after praying for help, she went to sleep.

Beth would graduate but Peggy and Irene had two more years to go, but the two girls were still Beth's oldest and best friends there at Mountain Mission School. Now that graduation was only a week away, Beth was mostly the school helper wherever she was needed, and she was still allowed to sit in on lectures. Also, she could still be a part of the choir, but she couldn't travel with the choir when they were on tour.

Mr. Brewster, a lawyer, had given one talk on Monday and would speak again on Tuesday afternoon. On Monday, he had given Beth an indication that she was the kind of person his firm would like to hire.

*If I had a job, then my biggest problem would be solved once I get away,* she thought as she went about her daily chores.

On Tuesday evening, everyone at the school was expected to attend a special event at the church and, of course, Beth would be present. Beth, however, wanted to talk to Mr. Brewster, today's lecturer, before he left the campus. Today he had said Beth could work for him when she graduated is she wished.

She needed to talk to him, but without being seen so she worked slower so that Irene and Peggy left before her. But now she was ready. When she reached the door, somebody called her name.

"Beth, come on," Peggy yelled as she started up the hill from the church. "I'll be there in about 5 minutes Peggy, called Beth. "I have to finish putting these roses in the small vases."

Peggy, Irene, and Beth had been sent down to the church to decorate for a wedding. Really it was a "renewal of vows" for the science teacher, Mr. Schermets and his wife.

This was just some new notion, which was a waste of time, as far as Beth was concerned. Beth often wondered how that nice Mrs. Schermets could stay married to that two-faced, bald-headed, lecher.

Well, if her plans worked out, she would only have two more weeks to ward off his leering smile and too-familiar hands. Beth shivered in disgust. Now, she had to wait until Mr. Brewster came down the hill.

"God, if you're really there, please, please let Mr. Brewster help me," prayed Beth silently.

Beth looked across the road at the big old water wheel that turned on and on without any help. *Just a small trickle of a stream ran under it, but that small trickle kept that big old wheel constantly turning. Just like life,* thought Beth. *A wheel in a wheel that turns perpetually as each life marches through its days and then it is renewed in another life. Here I am, 16 and ready to graduate, but still here because I have nowhere to go. Mr. Brewster's coming is like that little trickle of water that will get my wheel moving again,* thought Beth just as she heard the car crunching on the gravel as it came down the hill.

She knew that the car would have to go very slowly as it went by the waterwheel because of the bump over the grating. So, she quickly shut the church door and dashed across the road. She slipped behind the small pine that grew at the edge of the road. Sure enough, Mr. Brewster slowed to a near stop and Beth stepped boldly from her hiding place.

"Well, Hello, again, young lady," said Mr.

Brewster in surprise. "Where did you come from?"

"Mr. Brewster, did you mean it up there when you said you would give somebody like me a job?' questioned Beth in a hushed whisper.

Puzzled but wanting to help, Mr. Brewster said, "Yes indeed, I did. Are you interested in working for me?

Quickly, before she lost her nerve, Beth stuck out her hand, "Could you give me a card with your address on it, please? I might just take you up on that job offer."

Mr. Brewster reached in his pocket and produced the card which Beth grasped quickly and then smiled, "Thank you so very much, Sir. You can't know what this means to me," she said, still trying to smile.

"Well, let's hope we see each other again, Miss… Riley, isn't it?

With a broad smile, Beth turned, "Yes, it is. I need to go now, or they will send a search party to find me. Thanks! Then she darted across the road to the church as Mr. Brewster shifted the car into gear and went on down the hill.

Mrs. Goins, the Senior Advisor, was near the entrance when Beth made it back to the front entrance. "I was going to look for you. What happened?"

Beth smiled and dropped her head in a

regretful pose, "Sorry, Mrs. Goins, I guess I got to thinking about what I will do in another week and lost track of time."

Patting Beth's shoulder, Mrs. Goins said, "Aw now, you don't need to worry. You know you can have a job here. I know Mr. Schermets will put in a good word for you as well as about everyone else. Most girls aren't that lucky."

Inwardly shuddering, Beth replied. "Yes, I guess I am fortunate. It's almost dinner time, isn't it? My stomach is acting like it is," grinned Beth.

"Your clock is still working, I see," smiled Mrs. Goins. "Everyone knows your stomach can tell time and always has. Go on now and eat a good meal. Lord knows it doesn't make you fat."

So, Beth accomplished her task of setting up the first part of a get-away plan, undetected. Now she only had to wait until May 28$^{th}$ or perhaps find a quicker solution. There were still several arrangements that had to be made.

It would be wonderful if she could take Peggy and Irene into her confidence, but she was afraid to. She certainly could not tell Marlo because she was so naïve and innocent, she would be sure to tell everybody she met before the day was out.

Marlo thought everybody at Mountain Mission School was good and she trusted everybody who worked there. Marlo even trusted Mr. Schermets. *Well, he'll not bother Marlo, not while he thinks, I'm his 'Plum for the picking,'* thought Beth gleefully as she visualized Mr. Schermets' angry frustration if her plans worked out.

# CHAPTER 15

On Wednesday, Beth went into the dining hall, where she ate, laughed, talked, and helped clear the tables, without thinking about what she was doing.

She gave a startled jerk and almost fell when Jerry Curtis whispered, “Hi, Beth. Do you have to do all this by yourself?”

Beth regained her footing and stepped closer and lowered her voice, “Jerry, I hadn’t gotten everything planned when I first asked to go with you to Huntington, but now, I need to know. Could you take two passengers when you leave here next Thursday? Please.”

“Who?” Jerry wanted to know.

Beth hesitated for a moment and then said, “I need to trust you. Can I trust you, Jerry? I’m desperate,” pleaded Beth.

With a puzzled smile, Jerry bent to whisper in her ear, “You can trust me. Don’t worry. I won’t tell. I may not be able to take your passengers, but I promise not to tell anyone.”

“Jerry, I’m one of the passengers, but I can’t tell you about the other one yet,” explained Beth. She was almost in tears from her fear and desperation and Jerry readily picked up on that.

Jerry was excited about spending time with Beth and seeing her agitation as she clenched her hands together filled him with compassion. Before he thought about the consequences, he said, "Okay partner, we'll manage some way."

Beth was so thankful that she patted his hand lying on the table. She really wanted to hug him, but she had learned that hugging men could get her in trouble, so she hadn't done that since she was twelve years old.

Hesitantly, Beth touched his arm. "I'll pay you, but I don't have much money right now. Jerry, I wouldn't ask a favor like this from anyone, but this means more to me than anything in my life."

Beth worriedly looked around, "I can't talk now though. I'm expected in the church. I'll have it all worked out by Saturday so don't forget to come by the store at 10 o'clock, okay?"

Jerry patted her hand. "Relax, Beth. I'll help you. I always come to town on Saturday anyway and everybody who knows me is always kidding me about my Saturday trips. Nobody will think a thing about me stopping at the store, in fact, I may buy a shirt if I can find one that fits."

Beth smiled and hurried away leaving Jerry feeling like he'd won the sweepstakes. *She acted like she really likes me,* he thought as he hurried back to his truck with a smile on his face.

Beth dashed to the church, but she slowed down at entry. She quietly opened the door and made her way to the choir section. When nobody seemed to notice her entrance, she breathed a sigh of relief. Luckily, other people were also coming and going in their efforts to locate family members, which made it easier for her.

Peggy, who had the seat next to her leaned over and whispered, "Where were you? I was beginning to get worried."

Beth acted as if she hadn't heard at first and then whispered, "I'll tell you later." This satisfied Peggy, but Beth wondered what kind of excuse she could come up with later.

The Pastor of the church came to the podium, and everyone settled down as the introduction was made, and then the choir began their first song. Everything else was pushed to the back of Beth's mind. She loved singing with the choir.

The entire service was nice, but Beth wondered why Mrs. Schermets wanted to renew her vows with a husband like that sneaky, lecherous, hypocrite. Beth sat thinking *I don't think I want to ever marry. Marlo's dad beat her and killed her mother. Peggy's dad left her, and never came back. Mr. Schermets lives a lie with his sweet wife, and she thinks he's a saint.*

Then her own father's face appeared before her eyes, and she blinked tears away. She remembered how kind, gentle, and loving he had been, and just for a moment she thought she was going to give way to her threatening tears. *I can't do that,* she thought and swallowed them back.

As they left the church, Peggy grasped her hand on one side and Irene on the other as they walked up the hill to the dormitories. "What kept you so long, Beth? I told Irene that Jerry Curtis probably waylaid you. He's got a crush on you and boy does it show," said Peggy grinning.

Irene laughed as Beth's face turned red. "That was it, wasn't it? What did he say? You can tell us."

Thinking fast, Beth smiled and said, "I think he really likes you, Peggy. When I see him, you are all he talks about. He does say he's going after coffee, but he knows you work in the kitchen."

Irene raised her eyebrows. "If that's the case, then Peggy needs to ask him why he keeps his eyes fastened on you, Beth. When he comes to the kitchen and you aren't there, he gets a cup of coffee and hurries out, so I don't think it's Peggy he wants to see."

Peggy stopped. "Irene's right, Beth. He may talk about me, but only because he wants to be close to you. Even the cooks have noticed how he looks at you, Beth."

Beth turned red. "I don't want him to feel like that about me. I like him. He's a nice boy, but I'm not really interested in some boy caring for me in that way." Although she spoke the truth,

Beth knew that she would use his caring to her advantage if it would help her to get away.

# CHAPTER 16

The next seven days were so fraught with anxiety and worry that Beth had trouble sleeping. She had to sneak and pack most of her belongings and a lot of Marlo's that she hoped wouldn't be needed. *If we need to leave a few things that's what we'll do,* thought Beth as she snapped one suitcase closed. The filled cases were hidden under her bed where they wouldn't be seen.

Even though Beth had taken care of most everything she needed to do, she could not come up with a plan to get Marlo away without being noticed. *I certainly can't tell Marlo until the last minute,* thought Beth with a worried frown.

Marlo was not retarded, but she was slow in some areas and one area was that she could not keep a secret. What Marlo knew, everybody was sure to know within a short space of time.

This week, Marlo's curiosity led to another embarrassing incident at Mountain Mission School for Beth. She learned that Marlo had told the students at her lunch table that Beth had silk clothes in her dresser drawer.

Alfred Walker, a student in her science class had stopped her on the stairs as they went to class. "Your little friend, Marlo, has certainly whetted all our desires to know more about you. She says you have silk clothes hidden in your dresser. Is that so?"

Beth turned beet red and tried to step around him, but he blocked her way. "Of course, we all do wonder how you can buy such luxuries. Most of the students here get their clothes at the store across the street and they certainly aren't silk," said Alfred with a jeering snicker.

"Excuse me, Alfred, I don't want to be late for class," said Beth as if she hadn't heard his derisive words. When Alfred didn't move, she looked around for help and saw none. The other students had stopped to hear her reply or something since the stairs were completely blocked. Just as she thought of using the sharp edge of a protractor Benny Schaffer broke through the crowd.

"What's going on here? Beth, what's the matter?" Benny asked as he reached her side.

"Nothing is happening, Benny Schaffer. We only asked our star pupil how she can afford to buy new silk clothes when nobody else can," sneered Alfred.

Benny, who had grown from a hundred pound weakling with a stutter, to a six-foot-tall weightlifter with no stutter said, "I think you owe Beth an apology, Alfred. I want everybody to hear it, or you could have a bad fall on these stairs."

"No, Benny, he's just being stupid. Marlo ran her mouth with a bunch of foolishness, and they all believed her. It's not worth all this trouble," said Beth grasping his arm.

Benny was angry. "So be it. I'm leaving in about five days anyway," and he turned back to Alfred.

"What's it to be, Alfred? You need to pay for all the jeering and laughing you've done to me down through the years, anyway," said Benny.

"I . . . I was just telling what Marlo said, Beth, so don't blame me if she's a blabbermouth," said Alfred as he gave Benny a wary look.

Beth nodded and touched Benny's arm. When he looked at her, she smiled and said, "Let's all get to class before Mr. Schermets sends for us.

The whole class began to move, and Beth stepped to the side and waited for Benny. When the others had all gone ahead, Beth looked at Benny.

"Marlo must have told them something and Alfred has always been jealous of everybody. He thinks I have money, but my little allotment isn't all that much."

Benny smiled. "I thank God that I can get away from here as soon as we graduate. What are you going to do, Beth?"

"I can't go and leave Marlo, but I sure want to. I can't stand much more of Mr. Schermets," said Beth with a worried frown.

"If I could find some way to leave and take Marlo with me, I'd do it in a minute."

Looking up the stairs, they saw the science room door opening and Benny started on up the stairs. "Let me know if you need any help," he said and went on up the stairs. But Beth was right behind him.

When they reached the door, Mr. Schermets stood waiting with a scowl on his face. "Schaffer, what do you mean by loitering on the stairs? Why didn't you come on in with the other students?"

Benny stood looking down into Mr. Schermets face and then said, "I had something to tell Beth. Is that a problem?"

"What was so important that it couldn't wait until after class? Beth helps me arrange my materials," said Mr. Schermets as he turned back into the room.

Benny looked at Beth and raised his eyebrows in question. Beth frowned and lowered her eyes as she passed by Benny and went on into the room. *I'd like to trip that dirty swine and watch him fall flat on his face. Thank God, I only have a few more days in his class,* thought Beth as she quietly took her seat.

When class was over, and she started to leave, Mr. Schermets said, "Beth, I will need your help for a bit so please wait."

Beth looked startled and looked at Benny

with a troubled frown, but she turned to look at Mr. Schermets and said, "I'm sorry, Sir, but I've promised to help someone, and I don't wish to disappoint them."

Mr. Schermets looked stunned. "Is this someone important enough to jeopardize your chance of getting a job here when you graduate?"

Beth knew he wanted her to stay on and work for him, but she also knew that he wasn't aware of her knowledge. She hesitated for a moment and then she said, "I hope I'm not important enough that someone else couldn't replace me. I like to keep my promises."

"Who at this school is so important that they would be upset if you were a few minutes late?" asked Mr. Schermets in a querulous tone.

Benny had waited just inside the door and now he spoke up. "I'm the important person who needs her help and we need to leave now. Please excuse us. We do need to meet a schedule."

Beth looked at Benny and smiled. "I hadn't forgotten Benny. I'm sorry, Mr. Schermets, but we really do need to go." She reached out and took Benny's extended hand and went with him out the door.

At the top of the stairs, they were startled when the door slammed behind them, but they ignored it and went on down the stairs together.

"What do you think he wanted, Beth? He

talked like he had a job for you if you were to stay on after graduation. I thought you wanted to leave. You do, don't you?" asked Benny.

Beth looked around to see that nobody could hear them and then whispered. "Yes, I do, and I am leaving, but I need your help. Will you help me?"

"You know I'll help you. What can I do?" Benny asked. They were now at the bottom of the stairs and as Beth started to answer him, Mr. Schermets came down the stairs at a fast clip.

"I thought you two had a schedule, but it must not be important," he said as he passed them and went on out the door.

Benny grinned. "I'd say neither of us is his favorite student, wouldn't you?"

"You're not Benny, but he likes me better than I want him to, or something. I don't like to be around him alone," said Beth.

"That hypocrite! Has he done anything to you? If he has, I'll 'lay him out' on some dark night?" Benny was angry and Beth looked startled.

"No, Benny. He hasn't done anything except rub against me, pat my back and arms, and once tried to hug me. I'm wary, though and I certainly don't encourage him," said Beth.

"Does anyone know about this? They should if they don't," said Benny.

"I'm leaving, Benny. He doesn't know it

though and neither does anyone else. I'm going to take Marlo with me, and she hasn't graduated. That's why I need help," said Beth.

# CHAPTER 17

Benny and Beth walked slowly along the path leading to the dining hall. "How can you get Marlo to the store and into Jerry's truck without her knowing it? Marlo is bigger than you, Beth," said Benny.

Beth shook her head with a worried frown and pursed her lips together. Suddenly she stopped and grasp Benny's arm. "Benny, would you be willing to act like you are interested in Marlo? She likes you and I think if you asked her to go over to the store with you, she'd do it. If I can get her there, without her telling the whole school, it would really help."

Benny's eyes blared. "Beth, I know you love Marlo, but I don't want her to think I'm interested in her."

Benny stopped when he saw that Beth was upset. "Listen Beth, you don't know how Marlo acts if some boy/man pays any attention to her. She latches on like a leech and . . . well, she would drive me crazy."

Beth put up her hand. "Stop! I know she craves attention and probably gets carried away at times, but I can talk to her. She isn't stupid, even if you think she is. Marlo's had such a hard life."

Benny stood listening to her and then said, "Once I get her to the store, what's going to happen? I'm certainly not getting into that truck with her."

"Just forget it, Benny. I'll find some other way," said Beth in an angry voice. She started on down the path and Benny grabbed her arm.

"Wait, Beth. I didn't say I wouldn't help, but we need a better plan. What if you sent her a note to bring something to the store and I offered to carry it because it is heavy? I think she would come that way since she loves to help you. She wouldn't have time to tell anyone for I would take the note," said Benny.

Beth stopped and stood listening intently. "Yeah, that just might work. I can ask Jerry to let us put our suitcases and whatever you help her bring, into his truck. Then I could tell Marlo that she and I were going to deliver whatever it is to get her into the truck. She wouldn't have time to tell anyone and once we're gone, only you, I, Marlo, and Jerry are the only people who will know what happened."

Benny smiled and nodded. "So, what can you ask Marlo to bring? You probably need two bundles since she will need help."

Beth had stood listening and now shook her head. "It's a good plan except I have no idea what I could ask her to bring to the store."

Benny patted her arm. "Well, let's go eat. We'll both try to think of something. It would be nice if we had something that some school or company would want, but what?"

They went on to the dining hall without talking. They both looked so somber that Peggy came to meet them. "You two look like you've lost your best friends. Are you mad at each other?"

"No, nothing like that, but I guess you heard by now that we had a set-to with Mr. Schermets," said Benny looking at Beth.

"We did and I don't think he'll want me working in the science lab now," said Beth as they went through the line to fill their plates.

Peggy motioned for Irene and they both came to the table where Beth and Benny had chosen to sit. As soon as they were seated, Irene said, "Okay! Tell us what has happened. Are you both in trouble?"

Benny grinned. "We don't know, but I'm leaving here in a few more days, so it won't do him any good to expel me."

He gave Beth a pitying look, "Sorry my friend. I guess you'll have to get chewed out for the both of us."

Peggy shook her head. "We don't care about that. We want to know what Schermets got upset about."

Beth sighed. "It seems that Marlo gave Alfred Walker something to embarrass me with and he was having a field day with his cronies on the stairs going to class."

"Marlo is like a sieve. If she hears

something in her right ear, she tells it before it gets to her left ear. I just knew she was going to give you grief over something. What did you do?" asked Peggy.

Beth looked at Benny and grinned. "I didn't do anything, but when my friend, 'six-foot Benny' came upon the scene, Mr. Walker apologized nicely. He didn't do it quick enough though since Mr. Schermets was already at the top of the stairs wanting to know what was going on."

"I guess you and Benny got a scolding, didn't you?" asked Peggy.

Benny grinned. "I think he wanted to, but since I am so much taller than he is, he only asked, "What's so important that it made you late for class?"

Everyone laughed as they visualized Mr. Schermets having to look up at Benny Schaffer and Peggy said, "I bet it makes him feel small. . . but then, he is small."

"In more ways than one," piped up Irene, who was as wary of Mr. Schermets as every other female student in his science classes.

"Why hasn't someone reported him or has anyone reported him?" asked Benny looking at Beth.

"How can one report and verify his looks, his lingering pats, and his accidental stumbles into one of us where he lands in inappropriate places?" asked Peggy shivering in disgust.

"Yeah, the other teachers think he's the most saintly and caring teacher in the entire school, according to what Marlo heard when she was dusting the teacher's lounge," said Irene looking at Beth for corroboration.

Beth pursed her lips. "I certainly do not wish to work for him in the science lab. I'll leave the school first."

Peggy shook her head. "No, you won't. You won't leave Marlo and we all know Marlo would trust him, no matter what he did, unless he hit her."

Beth nodded. "I know, I know, and I don't know what to do about it."

# CHAPTER 18

From the day she had taken on the care of Marlo, Beth had begun to pray constantly to Jesus asking for his help to teach Marlo what she needed to learn.

So, after her talk with Benny, Peggy, and Irene at lunchtime, she silently begged Jesus for help in solving the problem, but it stayed on her mind the rest of the day.

She had asked Benny to help, but since he didn't want Marlo to think he was interested in her, Beth couldn't think of any way he could help.

When she reached the dining room that evening, Benny was already there.

"Beth, over here," called Benny from his table on the end near the outside door. He looked excited and Beth went straight to him.

"What is it? You look excited," said Beth standing in front of him.

Benny jumped up and put his hands on her shoulders. You may need to sit down. I think I have an answer to your problem and perhaps mine as well."

Beth put her hands on his chest and looked up at him with shining eyes. "Don't just stand there. Tell me!"

Benny, who had loved Beth from the day she first entered fifth grade and smiled at him, gripped her shoulders tighter and started to pull her into an embrace.

However, when he looked down into those trusting brown eyes, he dropped his hands and said, "What if I could fix it so that both Marlo and I could sneak away with you?"

Beth's eyes widened. "How? I mean, yesterday you said there was no way. What's changed?"

Benny grinned and grasped one of her hands before turning toward the line going by the lunch counter. "Let's go get our trays and come back to this table. That will make it easier to sneak out the side door without being noticed. We'll go to your 'spilling' tree and talk."

Several years before, Beth had told Benny about her 'spilling' tree when he found her crying while clearing the tables.

Alfred Walker had stopped on his way in the line and said, "The cooks know that you don't empty the scrap pails. I told them cause you think you're too good, Miss Prissy, but the cooks will report you," sneered Alfred but tried to change the sneer to a smile when Sally, the lunchroom monitor, told him to move on and not hold up the line.

Benny saw the whole thing and was trying to make her feel better. That's when she told him about the tree and Benny had kept the secret. Always, after learning about it, if he or Beth had a problem, the 'spilling' tree was their private place to talk.

Beth was excited today. They were meeting to talk, but not sad talk, she didn't think. Benny looked excited and she sensed that his news was good.

"Jesus, please let him have good news. I feel almost driven to get away, but I can't leave Marlo. She'd be in trouble before the week was out," mumbled Beth as she finished wiping the tables.

Both Benny and Beth rushed through the clean-up after the evening meal and hurried back to their dorms before slipping out the backdoors of each dorm and making their way to the tree.

Before she took a seat, Beth said, "Benny, I can't wait any longer. What is it? Is it good news?"

Around the backside of the tree, Benny sank to the ground pulling Beth down beside him. "I have a way to get Marlo away, but we will have to make some plans. You'll have to tell Jerry, but don't tell anyone else, especially Marlo," cautioned Benny.

"But how are you going to get Marlo down to the store without telling her something," said Beth with a worried frown.

"When you see Jerry this Saturday, just tell him to expect three passengers instead of two," said Benny.

"Three! No, no, Jerry told me he would have trouble taking two. Who else, is going?" asked Beth.

Benny grinned. "Me! You knew I was leaving and so does everyone else. Me going will not raise any suspicions."

Beth sat listening intently as Benny outlined a very intriguing plan. They went over and over all the particulars and finally satisfied that each of them knew what they needed to do for the next few days. They smiled like two conspirators and walked separate paths back to their respective dorms.

On Saturday, Beth told an excited Jerry that she would be accompanying him to Huntington on the following Thursday.

"Oh, that's great news, I can't wait," said Jerry smiling broadly.

Beth put her hand on his arm. "I'm taking Marlo Stevens with me. Remember, I told you that you would have two passengers?"

Jerry looked wary. "Is she in any kind of trouble? I can't afford to lose my job."

"She isn't in trouble, Jerry. It is just that she's supposed to stay at Mountain Mission until she graduates, and she hasn't graduated," said Beth with a worried frown.

"There. . . there's something else I need to tell you," Beth said uneasily.

Jerry's eyes widened in surprise. "What

else are you planning, Beth?"

Beth swallowed. "Benny Schaffer will be traveling with us. The school approves of him leaving, though. In fact, his going makes it easier for me to get away with Marlo," explained Beth.

"Somebody will have to ride on my bed then. Four people can't ride in one seat," said Jerry.

Beth looked startled. "That's right! I guess Benny didn't think about where he would sit." She shrugged in resignation.

"Benny's smart. I guess he has it all worked out. I don't think he would have told me otherwise," said Beth as they both turned to see Mr. Scales coming toward them. She smiled at Jerry and nodded at his approach before saying, "Okay then, I'll see you next Thursday morning."

# CHAPTER 19

Beth didn't see Benny until the following Wednesday and was worried sick. She was as ready as she could be without raising suspicion, but she was still uneasy.

Using several clever excuses, she had been able to get most of her possessions stored in an unused closet in the back of the store. However, packing Marlo's belongings had been difficult.

She missed lunch on two days with a 'supposedly sick headache' and went back to their room on this mission. She knew she'd have to leave at least two outfits of Marlo's clothing. It was difficult to get Marlo to decide what to wear each day. So, Beth decided that on Thursday she would go back to the dorm and grab whatever was possible and leave the rest.

All during the day on Wednesday, Beth's eyes roved every area of the campus hoping to see Benny. Since graduation, Benny had been asked to help in refurbishing the dorms and she knew he was busy. *He should let me know his plan. I don't know what to do or not do,* she thought worriedly.

She was busy in the lunchroom when Benny came in. She turned with a sigh of relief. "Oh Benny, I've been worried to death. Have you worked everything out?" she asked.

Benny nodded and took a seat beside her. "Tell me," Beth blurted out as he sat down.

"Do you remember that picture that did hang in the social room of the dorm? You know, it was of the waterwheel down at the entrance," asked Benny.

Beth thought for a moment. "Oh, the one painted by a former student. What's so important about that? Tell me what you've worked out."

Benny grinned. "That picture, my friend, has solved our problem. Well, it has if we can get Marlo to keep her mouth shut."

Benny explained, "The student who painted that picture has asked if she could have it and Mr. Wright has agreed. However, I just happened to be in the office when they were discussing the cheapest way of shipping it to Chapmansville, West Virginia. When I heard that town mentioned, my ears perked up. I'll not go into all the details, but they were very pleased when I told them that I was leaving Thursday and could take it since I would be passing through that town."

Beth's eyes lit up and then she shook her head. "Jerry isn't going to Chapmansville, Benny. He's going to Huntington," said Beth.

Benny grinned. That's Jerry's destination, but I can get off at the Chapmansville exit if I need to. Mr. Wright and the others know I'll be traveling with Jerry.

Beth smiled. "I guess you know that you

will have to ride in Jerry's bed behind the cab of his truck, don't you?"

Benny made a mock grimace. "No, my friend. I will not be riding in Jerry's bed. You and Marlo will have that honor."

"No we won't since Jerry will insist that I ride at his side," Beth said with a twinkle in her eyes as she smiled at Benny.

"Oh, I see. I have wondered how you enticed Jerry to break company rules about passengers," said Benny with a knowing grin.

"What are you two plotting?" said a voice and they both twirled around to answer.

"Mr. Schermets! You don't eat here. Did you need to see someone?' asked Beth hoping it wasn't herself.

Mr. Schermets put out his hand toward her shoulder and Beth automatically stepped back like a startled deer. "No, I don't eat here but your friend Marlo said you would be here, and I did need to see you," said Mr. Schermets as he dropped his hand.

When neither Beth nor Benny responded to this comment, Mr. Schermets straightened his shoulders and said, "I will be needing an assistant in the science lab, full-time, and I came to offer the post to you."

Beth hesitated. "I . . . I thought job postings were done on the first of the month. Isn't this early to be hiring?"

"That's true. The hiring is done on the first of the month, but I thought I'd check with you first since I know how capable you are. I wouldn't want anyone else if you are interested," said Mr. Schermets, smiling broadly.

Beth nodded." I thank you for your kind words, but I honestly haven't had time to make any plans for the future, yet. I have thought about college. I think I'll have to let you know. "

"You're getting started rather late if you are thinking of college. There's a lot of paperwork involved," said Mr. Schermets.

"Beth and I were just discussing attending Concord College and I know one of the professors there, so I don't think she or I would have a problem," said Benny moving closer to Beth.

Mr. Schermets gave Benny an angry glare and said, "I hope you are not trying to entice one of our best students into making a rash decision."

Benny stood for a moment looking calmly at Mr. Schermets. "Beth and I are best friends and have been since before you came here to work, Mr. Schermets, and I assure you that I would never, ever do or say anything detrimental to Beth Riley."

As if suddenly realizing that Benny may have closer feelings for Beth than just a friend, he turned with a smirk. "Young people often say things they don't carry out when tried by fire."

"Mr. Schermets I may be young, but I'm not devious and as you and I both know, some people are just that," said Benny in a very controlled voice.

Mr. Schermets turned red in the face and turned to walk away, but turned and said, "Let me know your decision by Friday, Beth. I hope you make a wise choice."

He then strode to the door and shut it with force as he left.

Beth threw her arms around Benny and looked up at him with a broad smile. "Benny, you sure put him in his place. I'll bet he goes to his next class and rakes every student there through the coals."

Benny hugged her as well and smiled. "As long as he doesn't get his way where you are concerned, I don't care how angry he is. He doesn't intimidate me."

# CHAPTER 20

Beth giggled as she listened to Benny's plan. "Alfred Walker will strut all the way to the dining hall bursting to tell me all Marlo said, but I won't be there."

"It is a good plan, even if I did create it," said Benny.

"I just hope that suitcase doesn't burst open on the way over that graveled driveway. Benny, I'm afraid to feel safe," said Beth with a worried frown.

Benny patted her shoulder. "The whole school will be aware that I'm delivering a picture for Mr. Wright, so they won't think one thing about Marlo helping me." He chuckled merrily.

"They will probably feel sorry for me since they are all aware of Marlo's tendency to latch onto a man if she thinks he is good-looking."

"I've heard some of the comments about Marlo being 'man-crazy' and I know she acts silly, but I don't know what to do about it," said Beth sadly.

"You'd think she would be afraid of men after the way her dad beat on her and her mother. When she first came here, she was afraid of everybody."

Benny shook his head still grinning. "Well, she isn't afraid now, but that's a good thing for our purpose today. Put it out of your mind, Beth. You have enough on your plate, right now."

So, at seven o'clock on Thursday morning, Beth was already at the store. She waited until just before she was ready to leave and then told Marlo to get up and get dressed. When Marlo grumbled sleepily Beth pulled back the covers.

"Come on Marlo, Benny Schaffer needs your help. He has a big package to take down to the store. He is leaving today, and he can't carry his suitcase and the package. I told him you would be glad to help. You will, won't you?" asked Beth and Marlo lit up like a candle.

"Sure, I'll help Benny, but where are you going so early?' asked Marlo.

"A new shipment is coming in today and I'm needed at the store and can't stay to help Benny," explained Beth and smiled at the eagerness with which Marlo was getting dressed.

Of course, both Beth and Benny knew that Marlo would pass the word around in the dorm and to anyone she met on the campus, that she, Marlo Stevens, was helping Benny Schaffer.

Beth thought that Marlo acted suspiciously on Wednesday night when she insisted that both she and Marlo took a shower and washed their hair.

"We only wash our hair once a week, Beth, and it isn't Saturday yet. What's going on?" asked Marlo.

Beth looked startled for a moment and

then smiled. "Graduation is coming up and lots of visitors will be coming to inspect the school which will cause a run on the bathrooms. I just think it will be safer for us if we get ours done so we won't be rushed if some special event is planned," explained Beth.

Marlo didn't seem satisfied though and Beth said, "Marlo, wouldn't you look better with clean hair if some really good-looking new male student suddenly enrolled?"

Marlo's eyes lit up. "You're right. This is the time when we get our new students, isn't it?"

Beth nodded and Marlo went happily to the bathroom leaving Beth to sneak a few more of her clothes into a grocery bag. She left before Marlo came out of the bathroom, but she yelled through the bathroom door, "Marlo, don't keep Benny waiting. He needs to be there when the truck arrives."

Going down the hill, Beth knew that Marlo would do anything to win Benny's approval, so she was satisfied with that issue. *I hope she doesn't get suspicious when we invite her to look at Jerry's little room behind the cab in his truck,* thought Beth as she arrived at the store.

Jerry was there waiting with a big smile on his face. "Good morning pretty lady, how are you?"

Beth smiled. "I'll be a lot better when we drive away from here. I'll need your help though to get away. Will you do me another favor, Jerry?"

Jerry's eyes blared warily. "What is it? I'm already breaking the rules by taking passengers."

Beth put out her hand to touch his arm. "Wait! Don't get all upset. I just want you to ask Marlo if she would like to look at your little room behind the front seat of your truck."

Jerry grinned. "Well, I can do that. I'll bet she don't know that truckers have that kind of set-up."

"Jerry, you will need to take her through the driver's side so you'll be ready to pull out as soon as Benny and I can jump in," said Beth anxiously.

Jerry's head jerked up in alarm. "Whoa! Are you kidnapping Marlo? If you are, I'm not getting involved in that."

Beth turned pale. "No, Jerry I am not kidnapping Marlo. She will want to go with me, but Marlo can't keep her mouth shut so I couldn't tell her. She thinks she is only coming down here to help Benny carry some things. She'll be really pleased when I tell her we are going on an adventure with you and Benny."

"Is she that stupid? I mean, most people wouldn't like for a truck to pull out when they were not supposed to be inside." Jerry had a stubborn look with his arms crossed in the front of his chest.

"Jerry, please. Benny and I worked this out, but we didn't have any way of letting you know about this part, or we would have told you. If I need to, I'll get back there with her," said Beth.

Jerry dropped his arms in resignation. "I've probably 'cooked my goose' and I do like this job, but . . . what the h . . .uh heck. This is an adventure."

Beth grasped both his hands and smiled and so did Jerry.

# CHAPTER 21

Soon Benny arrived with Marlo laboring along with her load right behind him. He stopped at the back of the truck and put his load down. "That thing is heavier than it looks when it's hanging on a wall." He worked his arms up and down a couple of times until Marlo stopped beside him.

Marlo smiled widely at Jerry. "I guess you're going to have passengers this time. Benny's going with you. I wish I could go somewhere, but I guess you get tired of all that driving."

Beth stepped back and nudged Jerry with her elbow. He turned to look at her and then realized the nudge was on purpose. He smiled and said, "No, but I have a room and a bed in my truck. I'll bet you've never seen anything like it. Do you want to see it?" he asked.

"Really! I didn't know trucks had things like that. Yes, I want to see it," gushed Marlo.

"You'll have to get in on the driver's side, but I'll help you up," said Jerry and then added, "But we need to get this picture and Benny's suitcase loaded first."

Having said that, Jerry opened his door and pressed a button on the dash, and then told Benny to lift the tailgate. They soon had everything loaded and Jerry said, "Come on, Marlo, if you want to see my sleeping quarters."

Beth was amazed at how quickly Marlo was inside the truck, she and Benny were in the front seat, and Jerry was shifting into gear to pull out onto the road. She, however, was not prepared for the ear-shattering scream that came from Marlo when she realized they were moving.

Jerry involuntarily jerked the wheel and hit the brakes as he skidded to a stop, but Beth said, "No, Jerry, don't stop. I'll handle this."

She turned and got on her knees in the seat. Her face was beet red, and she looked ready to burst. "Marlo, shut up!" she shouted. "Nobody is hurting you. We are going on a little adventure, that's all."

The scream had stopped before Jerry could get the truck going again. Marlo sat in open-mouthed awe as she looked at Beth. This woman looking at her had never shouted at her before so she must be serious. "Beth, why didn't you tell me if this is an adventure?"

"If I had told you, the whole school would have known it in five minutes. I couldn't tell you because you can't keep your mouth shut," shouted Beth.

She didn't realize she was shouting until Benny said, "Calm down, Beth. She's stopped screaming and Jerry and I aren't deaf."

Beth dropped her head into her hands and tilted backward when Jerry swung around a curve in the road.

"For God's sake, sit down, Beth. Jerry can't drive with Marlo's screaming, your shouting, and your butt blocking the windshield," scolded Benny.

Beth turned back and slumped into the seat burrowing her red face in her lap. She realized that she had been bound up like someone in a straitjacket, and Marlo's scream had caused her to lose control. Now she was shaking like a leaf in the wind.

Benny put his arm around her and said, "Okay, cry it out so you can relax. If you don't settle down, you're going to be sick."

Marlo leaned up over the back of the seat. "I'm sorry, Beth. I thought both of us were being kidnapped, but I'm glad to have an adventure and Benny will take care of us." She turned her head toward Benny with a big smile on her face.

"You will take care of us, won't you, Benny?" she asked.

"Marlo, when Beth calms down, we'll tell you about it, but we need to thank Jerry because he is the one taking care of all of us. Not me. I'm just delivering a picture."

"If I had known you were going to scream like a wild cat, I probably wouldn't have agreed to take you," said Jerry, glancing sideways at Marlo, and then continued, "If Beth hadn't said she wouldn't go without you, I would certainly not have helped you into my truck."

Beth was still shaking but seemed a bit calmer and Benny said, "Let's all just be quiet for a while and let Beth get all this behind her. I don't guess you happen to have a coke in your little room back there, do you," asked Benny.

"Yeah, there's one back there, but I can't stop on this crooked road. Marlo can look unless she's going to scream again," said Jerry.

"I'm sorry for screaming, Jerry. Here's a can of coke. Do you want it?" asked Marlo, handing it to Beth who still sat slumped in the seat.

Benny took the coke and opened it. "Here Beth. Raise up and drink this. Everything is calm now and you can relax."

So now that Marlo thought she was on a grand adventure, the inside of the truck became a jolly place to be. "Beth, I'm having the best time I've ever had. Where are we going?" asked Marlo in an eager voice.

Beth looked startled. "Huntington, I guess. Jerry, is Huntington your last destination for delivery today?"

Jerry's head jerked around and with a startled gaze, he said, "Do you really mean that you don't know where you're going? I thought you had someplace to go, or I wouldn't have brought you. What do you plan to do when we get to Huntington?"

"I'm going to find a hotel, get us a room, and then go looking for a job," said Beth as if it should be obvious.

With that remark, both Benny and Jerry looked startled. Benny spoke up first, "Beth, it doesn't work that way. You can't just walk in and say you want a job and start working."

"You may not get a job for weeks and if you don't, what will you do? Beth, I thought you were smarter than that," said Jerry with a worried frown on his face.

Benny nodded in agreement. "You may have a little money saved Beth, but food for two people is not cheap. You told me you had the promise of a job."

From Beth's shocked look, Benny said, "You don't have a job, do you?"

"No, but Mr. Brewster told me that he would hire me if I ever needed a job," said Beth, as if that made everything fine.

"Who is this Mr. Brewster and where does he work?" asked Jerry in a very skeptical voice.

Beth grabbed her handbag and began digging through it. "Here's his card. He is a lawyer, but he has two addresses. I don't understand . . .."

Benny grabbed the card from her hand and read aloud. "Brewster, Pendleton, and White, Attorneys at Law, 2021 West Main Street, Huntington, WV, and also 1237 East Virgnia

Avenue, Chapmansville, WV. These people have offices in both places, I guess. Since you need a job right now, you can't go to both places. You'll have to decide whether you want to go on to Huntington or stop in Chapmansville."

Jerry shook his head and slammed his horn button as a car suddenly swerved in front of him. Once everyone was calm again, he said, "You don't have anything in writing. Any man would give a pretty girl a business card. You shore don't know nothing about the world if you trust every man you see."

"He's an old man!" stated Beth as if Jerry was silly.

Benny grimaced and shook his head. "You're right Jerry. Beth Riley is green as grass when it comes to knowing whom to trust."

"Listen you two, I'm not as stupid as you think I am. I sat in on two lectures that Mr. Brewster gave when he came to Mountain Mission in May. During one of his talks, I answered some questions that he asked the students, and he told the class that I was the kind of person his firm was always looking to hire. In fact, he said that when I graduated, he would give me a job if I wanted one," explained Beth.

"Even if you find this man, his company may not have an opening right now, Beth. I'm sure he hasn't kept a job open just in case you happened to apply," said Benny.

"You don't know which city he is in. He could be in Huntington, but he could also be in Chapmansville," said Jerry.

# CHAPTER 22

On the next exit off the Interstate, Jerry pulled off and into the first filling station he came to. Once they had stopped, he looked at the girls. "If you girls need to . . . well, if you need anything, you'd better get out and take care of it. I've got a schedule to meet."

Beth and Marlo eagerly exited the truck and headed inside where they saw a sign designating restrooms and hurried towards it.

"They won't go off and leave us, will they, Beth?" asked Marlo.

"No, they probably needed to use the restroom as much as we did," said Beth as she hurriedly washed her hands. "Let's hurry and grab some chips, cookies, or something. It's been a long time since seven this morning."

Marlo looked at the clock on the wall. "Beth, it's one o'clock! It's no wonder I feel so hungry. Aren't you hungry?"

They entered the store and Beth headed for the snack aisle, but Benny stopped her. "No, don't buy anything, Beth, we are going to stop at the next exit. Jerry says there's a Denny's Restaurant at that stop and we can get a meal. I'm starved and I know you and Marlo are also."

Beth turned back toward the door. "Why didn't Jerry wait before pulling off the toll road if he knew there was a Denny's that close?"

Benny grinned. "He's filling the gas tank,

but I think he needed the restroom as much as anybody else and had to stop."

"I wonder what a truck driver does when he gets on that big highway and there are no exits. What do they do?' asked Marlo.

Benny chuckled. "Don't ask me. I'm not a truck driver."

Beth shook her head. "Marlo, don't you dare ask Jerry that? He doesn't know us that well and besides it would embarrass him and me as well. That's not the kind of question women ask of men anyway."

From Marlo's puzzled look, Beth said, "Marlo, there are just some things not talked about with men, so don't ask him."

"Benny didn't care, but he didn't know, either. I'd still like to know, though," said Marlo as Jerry motioned them back to the truck.

Sure enough, Jerry pulled off at the next exit and they all walked into Denny's almost as fast as they had gone to the restrooms. Beth looked at the menu and then pulled out her billfold. "These prices are pretty expensive, and I don't want to do dishes."

Benny put his hand on Beth's arm. "Don't worry. If you don't have enough, I'll help you." Beth gave him a puzzled look.

"You didn't know it, Beth, but the school paid me a small wage for helping Mr. Scales. I did that for the last three years and I've been saving my earnings," explained Benny.

Beth and Marlo looked surprised. "How come neither of us ever saw you working?" asked Marlo, and Beth sat thinking for a moment.

"So, that's why you never came to supper when construction was being done on campus," said Beth. "I asked you once, but you didn't tell me. Why didn't you want me to know?" asked Beth.

Feeling left out, Jerry interrupted, "Men don't tell everything they do or know. Women do that. Don't they Benny?" asked Jerry.

Benny shrugged his shoulders and grinned. "It just never entered my mind that you would want to know, Beth. It wasn't like I was going to spend my life working with Mr. Scales. Anyway, you were always off to some choir meeting, a play, or some honor society event. You didn't have time to even notice I was still alive, but you may not have known me anyway. I had to wear goggles and a hard hat when I was working."

Beth nodded. "Yeah, that's true. I was away a lot, but I always told you what I was doing."

Jerry broke in. "Are you two a couple? If you are, Beth certainly didn't tell me, or I wouldn't have helped her."

"A couple! What do you mean, Jerry? I'm not a 'couple' or anything else with anybody," stated Beth with an angry glare.

Marlo jumped in. "They ain't going together, Jerry. I'm with Beth all the time except at meals. They sit together then, but that's all."

Jerry looked at Benny who grimaced and nodded in agreement. "No, Jerry. Couples don't get together at Mountain Mission School. Beth and I have always been friends and I . . . well, I feel like I need to protect her. She's not big enough to protect herself."

Beth grinned. "I've made out pretty good so far, but thanks, Benny. I didn't know you were protecting me. Now, I feel much safer."

Just then the waitress came with their food and all bantering stopped as they enjoyed their first good meal of the day.

When they were almost through, Benny said, "Beth, let me run an idea by you and see what you think."

"What kind of idea, Benny? Whatever Beth does, I have to be in on it, you know," said Marlo.

"Yes, I know, Marlo, and that only makes my idea that much better. Beth must get a job, and a place to stay, and still watch out for Marlo. Am I right?" Benny looked at Beth, then Jerry, and finally Marlo.

"We all know that Benny, so quit beating around the bush," said Beth, and Jerry grinned as he nodded.

Benny held his fork in the air for a

moment. "Now, that card says Mr. Brewster's firm has an office in Chapmansville as well as Huntington, doesn't it? So, since I must stop in Chapmansville to deliver that painting, why don't you and Marlo stop there as well?"

"Is Chapmansville as big as Huntington, Jerry? I think a big city would probably have more opportunities for housing and work. Am I right?' asked Beth looking from one to the other.

Jerry shrugged his shoulders. "I don't really know, Beth, but getting this truck through Chapmansville is just as bad as it is in Huntington. What do you think, Benny?"

"Does it really matter about the size? What matters is that two young girls don't need to be set out all alone in either city. This way, I could find us two rooms in some hotel and then stay here until Beth goes to see Mr. Brewster and finds her someplace to live," said Benny with a worried frown.

Everybody had stopped eating and Marlo spoke up first. "I think we should do that Beth. I'm scared some strange man might beat on us."

Beth looked startled. "Marlo, we won't be speaking to any strange men. Well, I know I won't and you'd better not unless you want me to beat on you."

Benny laughed. "See, I told you my idea was good. I may even watch Marlo until you get your job."

Jerry put up his hands as if to ward off disaster. "You're braver than I am."

Jerry chuckled and looked at Marlo. "You'd drive a wooden man crazy, wouldn't you?"

"No, a wooden man wouldn't have a brain, so I couldn't drive him crazy," said Marlo giggling.

Beth had remained silent and then looked at Benny. "You said you had an appointment somewhere after you delivered that picture, so helping me might keep you from doing what you need to do."

"No, I don't have to be there for another week. That should be enough time to get you settled," said Benny as he resumed his eating and so did the others.

# CHAPTER 23

Beth was walking beside Jerry as they left the restaurant and he said, "Beth, he's right. I think you'd better take him up on his offer. It makes sense and I certainly don't want to set you out somewhere and drive away. Benny has some free time, and I don't, or I'd offer to do exactly what he is offering," said Jerry taking her elbow as they reached the truck.

Beth smiled. "I know you would, Jerry, and I do so appreciate what you've done already. I think I'll do what Benny says, so don't worry."

Jerry sighed happily. "You'll let me know when you get settled, won't you? I could maybe, occasionally, make a stop when I'm coming this way." Having said that, he helped Marlo back into her seat while Beth and Benny climbed back into their seats, and they were soon on the highway again.

Jerry said, "How will you let me know, Beth? I'll be worried to death, not knowing."

Beth smiled and said, "You write your address down, Jerry, and I'll send you a note." Then she suddenly stopped. "No, I can't do that. Somebody else could get your mail, and then they would know where I've taken Marlo."

Benny had been listening. "I'll send you a note, Jerry. Everybody knew I was coming to Chapmansville and I'll not mention Beth and Marlo, but you will have their address. Don't expect anything right away though for it may take a few days to get these girls settled."

Jerry looked at Beth. "I'm glad Benny is willing to help. I was about to park this truck and stay right here with you."

Beth smiled warily. "I'll be okay, Jerry, and I certainly don't want you to do something that rash. The company would arrest you for stealing their truck."

Jerry looked stunned. "They would, wouldn't they? I was going to do something, but since Benny is your friend...," Jerry was interrupted by Marlo.

"Benny's doing this for me, Jerry. I guess you didn't know that I helped him carry his stuff to the truck. Benny said he'd help me sometime. You did, didn't you, Benny?' asked Marlo with a wide smile at Benny.

Benny's eyes widened in surprise but since everyone was looking at him, he said, "I said something like that Marlo, but I didn't mean I was going to help you leave. Well, in a way I was since Beth wouldn't leave without you."

Marlo looked ready to cry and Beth said, "Marlo, that doesn't mean that Benny wouldn't help you. Does it Benny? He just meant that he needed your help since he was trying to help both of us."

Benny eagerly nodded. "Sure, Marlo, I guess I just didn't make it clear, but I did help you and Beth."

Marlo was all smiles again. "You did help me. Thank you, Benny. I'm glad I helped you."

It was twenty minutes later when they arrived at the Chapmansville exit and Jerry carefully pulled off the ramp into the evening traffic. "Where are you going, Benny? You said some store, didn't you?"

"I'm not sure what it really is, but it's on East Second Street. I think at the next light we make a turn onto Second Street. According to the directions they gave me, we turn right at the light and stay straight until we reach *The Artist's Corner.* It's a museum or something, but it's also a small restaurant," explained Benny peering through the windshield.

Sure enough, there it was and luckily there was a parking lot designated 'truck parking' on the left of the building. Jerry drove the truck into the lot and killed the engine. He turned to his passengers. "Here we are, folks. What do we do now?"

Benny looked at his watch. "It's three forty-five so I can deliver the picture and I'm sure they can tell us where a decent hotel that isn't too expensive is located. So, you girls stay in the truck while Jerry and I take care of the delivery. Then we'll go looking for a hotel and Jerry can make it on to Huntington without getting off his schedule."

Beth sighed. “I can’t believe we are here. Marlo, you don’t have to go to classes and clean all those dishes that you hated to wash every day. What do you think of that?” She looked at Marlo who looked troubled.

“What’s wrong, Marlo? I thought you hated doing dishes. Aren’t you happy to be on this adventure with me,” asked Beth.

“Where will we sleep, Beth? We don’t have a house and we don’t know anybody,” complained Marlo fearfully.

Beth turned her back to the street and got on her knees in the seat again, so she could look Marlo in the face. “Don’t be afraid, Honey. You know I’ll take care of you. I’ll find us a place to live, and we will be very happy. It may take a few days, but with Benny here with us, we’ll be fine. So, don’t get scared. I promise, we will be fine.”

This seemed to satisfy Marlo and Beth settled back into her seat to wait for Benny’s return.

“Are we going to live in this town, Beth? I think it’s pretty, but it is busy. Will we like it?” asked Marlo.

“I’d rather not live right in town, but we may have to until we get used to this place. I’d rather live outside of town, wouldn’t you?” asked Beth.

Marlo leaned up and linked her arms over the back seat and patted Beth’s shoulders. “I want what makes you happy, Beth. You've been so good to me. I don't think I could have made it without you when Mommy died."

Beth reached up to pat the hands on her shoulders. "I think the Lord put us together Marlo. You needed help and I needed to feel that someone needed me. So, I think we've helped each other."

Marlo sat silent for a moment. "I'm not smart, like you, Beth, but I'm not stupid. Some of the girls in my classes acted like I was an idiot, but my grades were as good as theirs. I think that I'm just too quick to speak when I shouldn't. I don't mean to cause any trouble though."

"I know you don't Marlo and I also know you are not stupid. You just want to be liked so much that you try too hard. I think. Some people don't care whether they are liked or not, and they don't understand the need to be liked or loved," said Beth.

"I want everybody to like me, Beth. Is that wrong? Boys act as if they like me, but when they get with the other students, they say silly stuff about me. Why do they do that, Beth?" asked Marlo in a sad voice.

"I'm sorry, Marlo. Some boys go through a silly age, I guess. By trying too hard, you may be acting differently from the other girls. I don't know, Marlo, but maybe you could try to not be so friendly around every boy or man that you meet," said Beth.

Beth turned back around and sat in her seat, and Marlo sat back in her seat. "Beth, I don't understand what I'm supposed to do. The preacher at the church at Mountain Mission School said, 'if you want friends you have to be friendly,' but you are saying I'm too friendly with boys or men. So, how am I supposed to act?"

Beth sat stunned for a moment. "Marlo, there's a difference between being friendly and being flirty, I think. I've not had any experience with men, so I don't really know. I thought you shouldn't have told Jerry to give you a hug. I wouldn't tell a man to give me a hug."

"He gave you a hug, Beth," said Marlo in an accusing tone.

"I didn't tell him to, Marlo. In fact, I don't want a hug from a man," said Beth.

"Benny hugged you and you didn't say nothing," said Marlo.

"Oh, you mean when you screamed and tore my nerves to shreds. He was just trying to make me feel better. Benny has been my friend for years, Marlo," explained Beth.

# CHAPTER 24

She was certainly relieved when the truck door was opened on the driver's side and Jerry asked, "Hasn't Benny come back yet? I helped him deliver that picture, but he went to talk to somebody about hotels. He's been gone for almost an hour?"

"He hasn't come out that door and that's where he went in," said Marlo. Jerry settled in his seat and looked at his watch.

"If he don't hurry, I'll not make it to Huntington before their closing time."

"There he is," said Beth. "He doesn't have the picture, so I suppose his mission is accomplished."

Benny opened the truck door and got in beside Beth. "Sorry for the delay, Jerry. Mr. Gladstone, who wanted the picture, was in a conference and I had to wait for his signature."

Jerry started the engine. "That's okay, but I need to get you fellers to your hotel and get this rig back on the road. Give me directions and I'll take you that far before I leave."

"It's Best Western Logan Inn, 47 Central Avenue. Mr. Gladstone said to go north three blocks and turn left onto Central Avenue, and it's about four or five blocks down that street," said Benny as Jerry pulled into the traffic.

When the truck pulled to a stop on the street in front of The Best Western Hotel both

Benny and Jerry jumped out and soon all their luggage was on the sidewalk.

Benny put out his hand, "Thanks, Jerry. I don't know what we would have done without you, and I will send you a note." He patted his pocket where he had put Jerry's address and smiled at Jerry.

Beth clasped both of Jerry's hands. "Thank you, thank you, thank you. When I get a job, I'll get Benny to send you some money for all you've done for us."

Jerry turned red in the face. "I'm afraid we'll never meet again, Beth, so I'm going to be daring." He suddenly swept her into his arms and gave her a crushing hug before releasing her. He then smiled and said, "That was my payday, so you don't owe me."

Beth was embarrassed, but she smiled. "You work cheap, Jerry. You'll never get rich like that."

"What about me, Jerry? Don't I get a hug?" asked Marlo and Jerry carelessly threw his arms about her shoulders. Marlo threw both her arms around his neck and kissed his cheek. Suddenly, she looked at Beth and turned red in the face. "Oops! I forgot. Sorry, Beth."

Jerry backed away with a startled red face. "Okay, bye then. Benny, take care of B . . . these girls and let me know."

Benny smiled. "I promise, Jerry, so drive

carefully man, and thanks again." They all stood waving a last farewell to the young man who had been a true friend.

Benny turned first and motioned for a porter waiting in the portico of the hotel. Soon all the luggage was loaded on a cart, and everyone was inside. "We will need to sign in, I suppose. I called from Mr. Gladstone's office and reserved two rooms. Yours is 201 and mine is 203, but they are side by side. The rooms with the odd numbers are on one side of the hallway and even numbers are on the other side," said Benny as they walked toward the check-in desk.

"How long did you tell them we would be here?" asked Beth looking around the lobby with pleasure.

"I just registered for one night, but we can ask for another night if you haven't found some other place before check-out tomorrow," said Benny and stopped before the desk.

They soon had their keys and were climbing the wide carpeted stairs to the second floor. There they stopped to stare around them and were pleased with the wide, clean hallway.

"If our rooms are as nice as this hallway, we've hit it lucky," said Benny as he opened his door.

Beth did the same and then poked her head back into the hallway. "Our room is great, Benny. How is yours?"

"Mine is great as well. Let's hurry and get settled in and then we need to discuss your future," said Benny.

"My future! What about your future? This is not your stop," said Beth.

"No, it isn't but get settled and then I'll come to your room, and we can decide what we should do next," said Benny as he closed his door.

Marlo was busy taking her clothes out of her suitcase, but Beth stopped her. "No, Marlo. Don't unpack. We won't be here very long so we can just live out of our suitcases for a couple of days."

"Where are we going? We don't have any other place to go, do we?" asked Marlo with a worried frown.

Beth patted her shoulder. "Not yet, we don't, but who knows what tomorrow will bring. I'll get a job and get us settled in, but let's not worry about it right now."

There was a knock on the door and Marlo jumped to open it. "Marlo, don't open the door! That may not be Benny," scolded Beth, but it was Benny and Marlo turned back to Beth.

"I knew it was Benny. He said he would come to our room, remember."

Benny turned toward the door. "See this chain with this little clasp on the end. This is a safety chain and every night you girls need to be sure this is in place on your door. Beth was right, Marlo. Don't ever open a hotel room door until you know who is on the other side."

Marlo tried out the clasp and chain and Benny came on into the room and took a seat in one of the chairs beside a table in front of the window. Benny sat waiting until Beth took a seat and then he pulled out a piece of paper folded in half from his shirt pocket.

"Mr. Gladstone gave me these directions to Mr. Brewster's law firm. He said he felt certain that the main office is here in Chapmansville. He wrote the directions here so we can find it easily," said Benny as he placed the paper in front of Beth.

Beth read everything carefully. "I think I'd better call the number on his card and see if I can get an appointment. Mr. Brewster is the one who offered me a job, so I think I should see him, don't you?"

"That's a good idea, Beth, but I don't think we can use this phone without paying for it, and we don't know how much it will cost," said Benny. Suddenly he picked up the phone and dialed zero and Beth sat still watching.

Soon Benny was talking to someone at the front desk. Benny ended the call and said, "There is no charge unless we make a long-distance call on the phone."

Beth jumped to her feet and grabbed the

phone from Benny's hand. "I'll call right now. What do I have to do? Do I just dial this number for the Chapmansville office?"

"You can try, but you may have to call the front desk and have them put the call through. We'll just have to learn all this by 'trial and error' since neither of us has any experience with hotels," said Benny solemnly.

Beth called the front desk first and told them what she wished to do and was told to dial 1 before she dialed the other numbers. In a few seconds, she was put through to the offices of Brewster, Pendleton, & White, Attorneys at Law.

# CHAPTER 25

Beth was answered by a receptionist who told her that Mr. Brewster was in the Huntington office for the rest of the week.

"He is scheduled to be here on Monday. Do you wish to make an appointment?" asked the receptionist.

Beth turned to Benny. "I think I should schedule the appointment, don't you?"

Benny was standing beside her, and he nodded in agreement.

"He's the man you need to see I think since he gave you his card," said Benny.

"I was hoping you could see him today though. Now we don't know whether to try to find an apartment for you and Marlo or really anything since you don't know where you'll be working, even if you get the job."

Beth scheduled the appointment for nine a.m. Monday morning and turned to Benny. "Benny, I have enough money to last us for several days if we're careful, so why don't you go on to wherever you need to be? We'll be fine," said Beth.

Benny shook his head. "No, Beth, I'm not leaving until I know what is going to happen to you. I wish you could have seen him today or tomorrow. Now we'll probably have to pay for three or maybe four more nights. This is only Thursday and then we'll have to buy food for the entire weekend." Benny had a worried frown on his face.

A muffled moan was heard from the bathroom and Beth gave Benny a startled look. Then her eyes blared widely. "Marlo, are you crying?"

When Marlo didn't answer, Beth opened the bathroom door to reveal Marlo sitting on the commode with tears streaming down her cheeks. "Why are you crying, Marlo? We're all right. Benny and I are just talking about how to manage for the weekend."

Beth bent down and hugged Marlo and pulled her to her feet. Benny had jumped to his feet and stood listening.

"Marlo, we have a room, we have money for food, and we are all safe, so don't start crying and making things worse," scolded Benny.

Beth started to defend Marlo and Benny gave her a cautioning look. "Come on and let's all put our heads together. What do you think we should do, Marlo?"

Marlo's eyes lit up and she washed her face and hurried back into the room. "I don't see why Beth don't call the number in Huntington. If she could talk to Mr. . . whatever his name is. . . he may remember her and . . . I don't know. It would be better than sitting here all weekend afraid to eat."

Beth, who had been standing behind

Benny's chair, turned and threw her arms around Marlo. "That's pure genius, Marlo, and that's exactly what I'm going to do."

She went back to her purse and pulled out the card and then suddenly stopped. "I can't call, though. Didn't the desk say there was a charge for a long-distance call?" She looked at Benny who nodded.

"Let's call the desk and see how much it will be to make just one call," said Benny and immediately picked up the phone.

When he saw Beth's worried look. "I'll pay for the call, Beth, so don't start counting your money again."

The desk informed them that the call would be added to their bill when they paid before leaving and the call would be less than five dollars. Benny turned with a smile on his face, "Okay, madame, make your call and I do wish you luck."

Beth took a deep breath and picked up the phone. When the receptionist answered, Beth asked to speak with Mr. Brewster. The receptionist hesitated for a moment and then said, "Are you a client, or someone needing help?"

Beth explained her desire to speak to Mr. Brewster and the receptionist asked, "Are you here in Huntington?"

"No, I'm in Chapmansville and I called the

office here and was told that Mr. Brewster was in Huntington and would not be back until Monday. If I was assured of a job, I would know what to do about finding a place to live," explained Beth.

There was a pause on the line and Beth thought the call had been disconnected, but then a male voice spoke. "Ms. Riley, this is Hubert Brewster. I understand that you are looking for work."

Beth was bereft of words for a moment. "Mr. Brewster, do you remember me? I was the student at Mountain Mission School that spoke with you about a job. I stopped you as you drove past the water wheel at the entrance."

"Ah yes, the water wheel! I remember you. I did promise you a job or at least an interview, didn't I?" asked Mr. Brewster.

"Yes, Sir. I kept your card and that's how I was able to make this call," said Beth with a voice choked with tears.

When Mr. Brewster didn't speak for a moment, she gave Benny a helpless look, but when he spoke again, a smile brightened her face.

"Ms. Riley, would you rather live in Chapmansville or are you willing to live in Huntington? The position that is open right now is here in Huntington. We'll have to check you out and let the board members interview you, but I think you could fill this position," said Mr.

Brewster.

"I could live in Huntington, Sir, but I don't know how I can get there. I came here in a supply truck," said Beth.

She heard a chuckle on the other end and then Mr. Brewster said, "You're just like that water wheel, nothing is going to stop you on life's journey, is it?"

Beth laughed. "I hadn't thought about it, Sir, but I have kept on moving. I'm not ready to quit, that's for certain."

"Ms. Riley, where are you calling from? I need to work out some logistics and then I can call you back. How does that sound?"

Beth gave him the name and number of the hotel and her room number and was assured that she would receive a call that night or early the next morning. Beth slowly put the phone back in its cradle and then threw her arms around Benny.

"Benny, I believe I have a job! He's going to do something, but I think I'll be working in Huntington," whispered Beth since Benny was hugging her so tightly that she could barely breathe.

Beth pushed back to free herself. "Sorry, Benny, I shouldn't have done that. I was just so excited." Her face was suffused with color.

Benny grinned. "I wouldn't mind you getting excited more often if that is your reaction." Beth became redder and she turned her face away.

Marlo was standing with her mouth agape. "Beth, you said you wouldn't hug Jerry, but you just hugged Benny. What's the difference?"

Beth dropped her head. "I know, Marlo. I'm sorry. I just got so excited, and I knew Benny would be, too."

Benny realized that Beth must have been talking to Marlo about her actions around men. He said, "Marlo, I used to stutter and lots of our classmates laughed at me, but Beth didn't. So, she has been my friend like she is being your friend and friends can hug friends. Beth was not acting inappropriately."

Beth went on into the bathroom and closed the door. Just as she washed her hands, she heard the phone ring.

When she opened the door Benny was on the phone. As she hurried toward him, thinking it was Mr. Brewster, Benny said, "That's fine. Yes, we will want to be called in time for breakfast."

# CHAPTER 26

At eight a.m. the next morning, the telephone by the bed rang and scared both Marlo and Beth. They hit the floor at the same time with blaring eyes, but when the phone rang again, Marlo fell back on the bed. Beth answered the telephone. It was Mr. Brewster.

"Ms. Riley, can you be ready to leave in an hour? Mr. Palmer, who works in my office there in Chapmansville, needs to come to Huntington today, and he will come for you at nine o'clock," said Mr. Brewster.

Beth stood in shock for a moment but pulled herself together and said, "Mr. Brewster, two other people need to ride to Huntington with me. It is a long story, but without their help, I wouldn't have gotten here at all. So, if I come to Huntington, they will have to come with me," explained Beth in a fear-filled voice.

There was silence on the other end for a moment and Beth held her breath while waiting. Finally, Mr. Brewster said, "Mr. Palmer has a station wagon so two more passengers shouldn't be a problem. I suppose I should call him and tell him to give you another hour to prepare yourself or rather yourselves since there are others. There is no need for me to tell you that I'm anxious to hear this story."

"Oh, thank you so very much, Sir. I don't know what I would have done had you said no," said Beth in a more cheerful tone.

"That sounds better, so prepare for departure by ten a.m. since Mr. Palmer will want to get back to Chapmansville by four o'clock this evening," said Mr. Brewster and ended the call.

"Marlo, get up and get dressed. I'll go knock on Benny's door and you hurry and use the bathroom since I'll need it too," said Beth as she headed for the door.

Benny was up and dressed and delighted with the news. "It couldn't be better. Jesus truly heard my prayers last night. I do need to be in Huntington by tomorrow and I wasn't going unless I felt that you were safe and settled," said Benny.

Beth looked at him narrowly. "Benny Schaffer, why all the secrecy? I always tell you everything."

Benny pursed his lips. "I need to take some tests tomorrow, and I didn't want to tell you, just in case I failed. Beth, I'm trying to get a four-year scholarship to West Virginia University."

Beth's eyes lit up and she started to hug him but quickly stepped back. "I want to hear more about this, but we all must be ready to leave by ten o'clock and I'm not dressed."

Benny grinned. "Well, go girl. Get a move on, shake a leg, or whatever the modern saying is for people our age," said Benny pushing her out the door.

They made sure they hadn't left anything and went down to the lobby to wait for Mr. Palmer. He was walking toward the desk as they stepped into the foyer.

"I'm here for Miss Beth Riley" . . . he didn't get to finish because the clerk pointed behind him, as Beth walked forward.

Having heard their conversation, Beth stepped to the front. "Good morning, Sir. You must be Mr. Palmer. Am I correct?"

Mr. Palmer looked stunned for a moment. "I . . . well, I assumed that you were an older lady with two companions."

"I'm sorry, Sir, but I am Beth Riley, and my friends are Benny Schaffer and Marlo Stevens. Mr. Brewster wanted me to come to Huntington today. He said you were making a trip to Huntington today and he would work things out. I thank you so much for being willing to take us with you," said Beth.

Mr. Palmer smiled. "I have plenty of room in my station wagon and I don't mind company. Is this all the luggage you have?" A bellboy, pushing a cart loaded with luggage, came from the elevator at that moment.

Benny laughed. "That, Sir, is all our luggage. We've just graduated and left our school, so everything we own is before you."

Mr. Palmer stood looking at the loaded cart. "I believe we can get it all in the storage area, but we may have to put down a back seat."

"Do we have to sit on our luggage?" asked Marlo with a stubborn look on her face.

Beth saw the look and laughed. "If anyone needs to sit on luggage, Marlo, I'll volunteer. I just want to get to Huntington."

Mr. Palmer smiled. "Well, roll that cart out front for us, young man, and we'll see about cramming it into my station wagon."

They didn't have to put down a seat, so Beth smiled at Benny. "Since you've been so helpful and such a good friend, Marlo and I will let you have the honor of a front seat."

"Is he a better navigator than you, Ms. Riley?" asked Mr. Palmer, as they pulled onto the Interstate highway.

Beth laughed. "I doubt if either of us is very good since we have never traveled before. You could say that this is our maiden voyage."

Mr. Palmer glanced at Benny in astonishment! "You've graduated from high school and have never traveled! I don't understand."

Benny looked back at Beth with raised eyebrows. "We were raised in an orphanage, and it has its own school. Children can be taken there as babies, and they stay there until they graduate or become eighteen years old."

"I've never heard of it. Where is it located?" asked Mr. Palmer.

Benny hesitated after Beth tapped his shoulder. "Mr. Palmer, we would rather nobody knows where we came from. We aren't in any kind of trouble, but we felt that we needed to leave."

Nobody said a word for several seconds and then Mr. Palmer said, "I don't understand, but 'if you say so,' I don't know anything about any of this and never met you at all."

Benny sighed. "Thank you, Sir. Later, we can properly thank you, and we won't forget your kindness."

"I thank you as well, and I'm sure Marlo does also, but we need to be rather reserved for a few months. The Lord has eased the way for us in this endeavor and put people like you in our path. So, I, along with Benny, again thank you, and we do so appreciate you giving us a ride," said Beth in a tear-choked voice.

Marlo spoke up, "That sign said, Huntington. Are we already there?"

"We're in the city limits, but it will be a little slower getting to the offices," said Mr. Palmer, making a left-hand turn when the light turned green.

Four minutes later, Mr. Palmer slowed and turned right into a paved parking lot beside a tall brick building. "Here we are, folks. Leave your luggage and follow me. I need to see Mr. Brewster first anyway, so I'll take you to him."

On the ground floor, they entered an elevator and soon stepped out on the second floor facing a glass-fronted wall. Running across the front of this wall in six-inch letters was Brewster, Pendleton, & White, Attorneys at Law which reached the entire length of the hallway.

# CHAPTER 27

Mr. Palmer walked to a wide door set in the middle of the hallway and opened it. "Let's go meet the head honcho."

Since Beth was the person looking for work, she took the lead, and soon they were all inside and standing before a wide desk. The lady behind the desk looked up. "You made good time, Mr. Palmer, and you've brought all the adventurers, I see."

She turned to Beth. "I'm Nancy Jackson, the receptionist and general 'dogsbody' for this outfit, and you are Beth Riley, I presume." She had risen from her seat and now held out her hand.

"Ms. Riley, I've heard a lot about you. Who do you have with you?" asked the receptionist.

Beth smiled and shook the offered hand. Nodding at Benny she said, "This is Benny Schaffer, a classmate of mine, and this girl is my adopted sister, Marlo Stevens."

Ms. Jackson smiled and nodded at Marlo and Benny before turning back to Beth. "All of you take a seat and I'll see if Mr. Brewster is free."

She took her seat behind the desk and punched a button before saying, "Mr. Brewster, Mr. Palmer has arrived with his passengers." She listened for a moment and then nodded to Mr. Palmer.

"He wants you to bring them on in, Mr. Palmer."

As Beth walked behind Mr. Palmer, she felt so shaky that she grasped Benny's hand. He squeezed her hand and smiled, as he whispered, "You got this, Beth. I'm right behind you."

Marlo nudged Beth with her elbow. Beth turned to look at her, "What is it? I'll need to concentrate, so please wait."

Marlo looked down and Benny stepped up beside her. "Marlo, Beth is a nervous wreck right now, so please don't do anything to worry her. What do you need?" asked Benny.

Marlo raised troubled eyes to Benny. "I'm scared. What if I break something or spill something?"

"Don't touch anything, Marlo. Just sit down when we are told to, and please don't start talking," mumbled Benny, fearing Marlo might blurt out, 'We've had an adventure. We ran away from Mountain Mission School.'

Mr. Brewster rose from his seat as they entered and extended his hand. "I can't recall your first name, but I do remember your beautiful hair and that your name is Riley. I also remember that you had a quick intellect in getting to a solution for a problem. That is why I told you we would be interested in hiring someone like you. I'm glad you decided to come."

Beth shook his hand. "My name is Bridget

Elizabeth Riley, but everyone calls me Beth. I thank you so much for seeing me today and for helping us with transportation."

"Who are your traveling companions, Ms. Riley? I'm interested in hearing your story," said Mr. Brewster.

Beth looked at Benny and said, "This is a classmate of mine, Benjamin Jefferson Schaffer. He is also the best friend I've ever had since losing my parents, and this is Marlo Stevens, my adopted sister, and I take care of her."

Mr. Brewster shook hands with Benny as he smiled and said, "Were you named for Benjamin Franklin and Thomas Jefferson?" Benny looked surprised but smiled.

"I was, Sir. How did you guess?" asked Benny with an impish grin.

Mr. Brewster shrugged his shoulders. "I've never heard those two names together in one name before, and I thought your parents must have been history buffs."

Benny smiled. "I've been told that they were, Sir, but I never knew my parents."

Mr. Brewster nodded and then turned to Marlo. "So, this beautiful lady is your adopted sister. How does one adopt a sister?" he asked as he put out his hand to Marlo who placed her hand in his with a wide smile on her face, but she didn't speak.

Beth smiled at Marlo. "She was brought to

the school in similar circumstances to mine and 'in my heart' she became my sister. I could not and would not leave without her.

Mr. Brewster gently dropped Marlo's hand and said, "Well, all of you take a seat and we'll see what can be worked out."

He turned to Mr. Palmer and said, "Thanks, James. If you will wait in the outer office, I'll be with you in a few minutes."

When Mr. Palmer left, Mr. Brewster said, "Even if I have a job for you, Ms. Riley, you will still need a place to live. What about your friends? Will they be living with you?"

Beth looked startled and looked at Benny. "I won't be staying with Beth, Mr. Brewster. Tomorrow, I'm due to take a test to see if I'm eligible for a four-year scholarship to West Virginia University. If I'm accepted, I will be living in Morgantown, but if I'm not accepted, I'll find a job and get my own place."

Mr. Brewster nodded. "You'll still need a place for tonight." Then he turned to Marlo, who dropped her head.

Beth spoke up. "Marlo will live with me, but I'd like to find a job for her also. She likes helping people cook and clean. She does not want to go to school, and I will not leave her by herself."

Mr. Brewster rose from his seat. "I need to see Mr. Palmer and check on some things. While

I'm away, you two girls can be thinking about what you would like to do. Benny needs to come with me and bring your luggage into a storage area that we have downstairs. We will be back in about twenty minutes."

He and Benny left the room and Beth jumped from her seat and hugged Marlo.

"Marlo, we're safe and I may have a job so we will have something to live on. Oh Marlo, to think that I thought I hated Jesus makes me so ashamed. Look what he has done for me and you! I wish I could let him know how ashamed I am and how I wish I could thank him," said Beth as she held Marlo with tears streaming down her face.

Marlo pulled back from Beth's embrace. "Beth, my mommy used to say that evil is loose in the world, and we are blessed if we make it through life without a few knocks and bumps along the way."

Then suddenly, as if she had forgotten their situation, Marlo said, "Do you reckon that is why she stayed with Dad until he killed her?"

Beth sat back in her seat, stunned for a moment, but when she saw the look on Marlo's face she said, "I don't know Marlo. Maybe your mom didn't have any skills and couldn't get a job where she could keep you with her. She is right though, about being blessed if we survive the knocks and bumps. Things happen that are so painful, but Jesus always gives us enough of whatever we need to help us survive. I think your mom's only concern was you, and she didn't care what happened to her."

Marlo held Beth's hand and looked so sad. "I remember Mom saying that her parents ran her off when she met Dad. I guess they wouldn't let her come back to them, or maybe Dad wouldn't let her go. He was a mean, mean man."

Beth patted Marlo's hand. "Yes, he was Marlo, but Jesus sent you to me. We've gotten along well, haven't we?"

Marlo hugged Beth and then sat back. "Yes, and now we need to be talking about what we want to do. I would like to find a job where I could do cooking and cleaning. I know how to do things like that, and I don't get nervous when I'm doing something I like."

Both girls sat quietly thinking until the door opened and Mr. Brewster and Benny came in. Benny stopped in front of Beth.

"You look like you've been crying. What's wrong? I thought you'd be on 'cloud nine,' after all that has just happened to you, Beth," said Benny In a chiding manner.

"It wasn't sad crying, Benny. Beth was just wanting to thank Jesus for helping her find Mr. Brewster and maybe get a job," said Marlo.

She had a wide smile on her face as she continued, "And I know what I want to do, so we haven't wasted our time."

Mr. Brewster had gone to his seat behind his desk and sat listening to Marlo, but he was studying Beth.

"So, now we know what Marlo wants to do, Ms. Riley, but what do you want to do?" he asked and sat quietly waiting.

Beth drew in a long breath. "I need to work so I can find a place for us to live together, but I can't leave Marlo alone while I am working. Are there such things as boarding houses or rooms where a person could pay their rent by working in the house?"

Mr. Brewster gave Beth an intent look and said, "You've told me what you think you need, but you haven't said what you want. I want to know about that hidden desire that you've talked to Benny about from an early age. Tell me what that is, Ms. Riley."

Beth gave Benny a startled look. "Benny, you shouldn't. . ." She was interrupted by Mr. Brewster. "Don't get upset with Benny. If he hadn't told me, I would possibly not have come up with the answers to your problems. Benny says your dream has always been to go on to college to become a teacher or a lawyer. Is that still your dream, Ms. Riley?"

Beth turned red, "What I want is not as important as finding a home for Marlo and seeing that she is safe. I promised her when she was brought to the school that I would never allow her to be hurt again, and I intend to keep that promise." Beth gave Benny a stubborn glare and then turned to Mr. Brewster.

"Benny has always known that Marlo came first with me, so he shouldn't have said anything."

Benny stepped toward Beth, but Mr. Brewster said, "No, Benny, wait until I explain the results of your supposed indiscretion."

Benny stepped back and took a seat beside Mr. Brewster's desk.

"All right, Ms. Riley . . .uh, may I call you, Beth?" asked Mr. Brewster and Beth nodded but still looked upset.

Mr. Brewster pulled his chair closer to his desk and picked up a pen. He wrote something on a legal pad and then looked at Beth.

"Did you know that Marshall University is just down the street from these offices?

Beth's eyes lit up. "I knew it was in Huntington, but I didn't know its exact location."

"Our board has discussed this position and now I think it is time to try it. I need an aide here in my office that would be a liaison between this law firm and the university. If you should be hired in that position, you could attend the university as a student and still do your job for me. Do you think you would be interested in something like that?" asked Mr. Brewster.

# CHAPTER 28

Beth's eyes lit up as she sat forward in her seat. I would like it very much, I think, but what sort of relationship does your firm want with the college? Depending on what it entails, I may not be a good fit."

Mr. Brewster smiled. "Ah ha! There's that creative thought pattern that I recognized when I was at Mountain Mission School."

The three 'escapees' gasped when he said Mountain Mission School, but Mr. Brewster expected that reaction and smiled.

"Don't be alarmed. I knew you were all from Mountain Mission School even though I had only met Beth. I want to hear the whole story, but right now let's talk employment."

"Our firm would like a relationship with the university to assure us that students who graduate with law degrees from the university have mastered all the rudiments to become reputable lawyers, who are grounded in the confines of the laws in each state as well as nationally. We want people seeking lawyers to think of the university as 'the place to go' to find qualified lawyers. We also want companies looking to hire lawyers to check with the university first before looking elsewhere." Mr. Brewster talked as if he was 'thinking aloud' or 'visualizing' as he spoke.

Beth had watched him intently and now

spoke. "Mr. Brewster, have the other members of your firm agreed on this concept or is it so new that it hasn't been discussed?"

Mr. Brewster's eyes lit up. "There! That's what I remember about you. You are very perceptive, Beth. I like your quickness in detecting holes in an issue."

Mr. Brewster hesitated for a moment. "The board is aware of our plan and my partners want the same things that I've just explained. However, nothing has been nailed down yet. We hope that whomever we hire will help us fill in those 'holes' that need to be filled."

Then, as if he was finished, Mr. Brewster sat back in his chair and looked at Benny.

"I think Benny has some news for you girls and I'll leave him to it." Mr. Brewster rose to his feet and walked around his desk. He stopped in front of Beth.

Beth rose as well with a perplexed look on her face. Mr. Brewster nodded at her and said, "Beth, the Board will interview you, tomorrow at eleven o'clock. So, tonight you need to devise an operating model for this new program and be prepared to explain your ideas to the board."

Beth gasped in surprise. "I don't think I can do that, Mr. Brewster. I'm not conversant in legal terminology and I certainly have never spoken before a Board."

Mr. Brewster gave her a gimlet stare. "I

thought you had come to Huntington to find a job. Being interviewed is a requirement for any high-paying job, Beth. Were you not aware of that requirement?"

Beth dropped her head. "I think I've been very unwise, but I really needed to get away from Mountain Mission School and I took the first opportunity I could find."

"Is the school that bad? I was impressed when I was there and you are certainly well educated," said Mr. Brewster in a puzzled voice.

The three 'escapees' all gasped in shock and Beth said, "No, oh no, Mountain Mission School is wonderful. There could not be a better environment for children who don't have their parents. I loved living there and appreciate that school so very much, but I had a reason for wanting to get away," said Beth.

"Mr. Brewster, none of us left because we didn't like the school. It is a super school, but Beth and I have graduated and needed to leave and find our place in life, and Beth would not leave without Marlo," explained Benny.

"That nasty old Mr. Schermets is the reason" ...Marlo stopped. "Oops! I forgot, Beth. I'm sorry."

Benny gave Marlo a threatening look and Beth turned red and dropped her head. The room was totally silent for a moment and then Mr. Brewster said, "Never mind, Beth. Since this has been such a stressful day and you haven't been to your hotel yet, I'll reschedule your interview for four o'clock tomorrow afternoon."

Beth looked at Mr. Brewster with a troubled expression. "I do need a job and I would love to work for you, but I feel like I've been tossed into the ocean and I'm not a good swimmer."

"That's what we want, Beth," said Mr. Brewster but Marlo's eyes blared angrily.

"You talk like you want Beth to drown," said Marlo looking ready to do battle.

Mr. Brewster looked startled for a moment and then chuckled. "I guess that did sound like I wanted to drown her, Marlo, but I would never do anything to harm your protector."

Mr. Brewster looked at Beth. "I think I didn't explain the situation very well. Our firm has been trying to work with the university, but we aren't getting the results we hoped to find. Hiring someone like you who will be a student, and therefore begin on the 'ground floor' so to speak, who we hope will have innovative ideas that will get our project moving in the proper direction. We just want your ideas or thoughts about the best way to accomplish our goals."

"What if my ideas aren't any good or not what you were looking for," asked Beth, who now had an interested look in her eyes.

"I'm being honest with you, Beth. This is

why I've been here in Huntington practically all week. I've discussed this with the college administration, several students, several teachers, and members of our Board. Before I had any idea that you were anywhere in the area, we had decided to post this position," said Mr. Brewster, giving Beth a steady look.

So, you really needed to see my ideas on what you had visualized before you returned to Chapmansville, didn't you?" asked Beth.

"Yes, I did, Beth. If you are found to be satisfactory by the Board then we will have no need to post the position. You will not be expected to implement any of this on your own, and there is no rush to lay the groundwork," said Mr. Brewster.

Beth rose to her feet. "You've given me a challenge, but I accept. I'll do the best I can. However, with not knowing where Marlo and I will be living and so many other things that are boggling my mind, I fear that I can't concentrate as I should."

Mr. Brewster rose to his feet as well and looked at Benny. "I think your friend, Benny, has taken care of your hotel for four days. That should help some. If you are hired, then Ms. Jackson and some of the other staff will help you, so try to not worry about that until next week. I feel like everything will work out just fine."

# CHAPTER 29

A taxi took Beth, Marlo, and Benny to a hotel three blocks from the office and they were soon settled into two rooms, located on one side of a long hallway.

As soon as they were settled in, Beth took the legal pad given to her by Nancy Jackson and seated herself in one of the two chairs at the one table in the room. She sat staring without seeing anything. *I need to think, but all I can do is fret about where Marlo will stay while I'm being interviewed*, she thought tiredly.

Benny knocked on the door, and after telling Marlo who he was, she opened the door. "See, Benny. I did as you said, didn't I?" asked Marlo, smiling brightly.

"You did good, Marlo, but now you need to help me to help Beth. We need to not bother her, so she can concentrate. We do need to eat though, so if you girls are ready, we'll go out to eat and I'll pay if you don't eat too much," said Benny, chuckling at Marlo's look.

"Benny, I can't leave Marlo alone tomorrow while I am being interviewed. What can I do? You'll be taking your test and I won't leave her here in this room alone," said Beth.

"Beth, calm down! Marlo can take a book or a crossword puzzle with her and wait in the office with the receptionist. I'm sure Ms. Jackson won't mind," said Benny,

"I'll stay with her, and I won't talk, Beth, so you don't have to worry about me," said Marlo as if bestowing a favor.

Beth smiled. "Do you promise, Marlo?" Beth knew that if Marlo promised she would try her best to keep that promise.

Marlo nodded and said, "Yes, Beth, I promise."

Benny smiled. "Okay! Now, let's go out and eat. I thought about bringing food here, Beth, but if I did, you would try to work and eat, and that isn't good for you. It won't take more than an hour and when we get back, I'll talk it over with you. Sometimes discussing things with someone else gives one a different perspective and that can be helpful."

"We don't have enough money, do we, Benny? We have our rooms for four days, but we can't splurge on food," said Beth.

"That's something else we need to discuss, but let's go eat, first. I can't discuss anything on an empty stomach. There's not much of you to fill up, but it takes quite a bit to fill me," said Benny," stretching up as tall as he could.

They walked down the street to a McDonald's restaurant and soon were happily enjoying hamburgers, fries, cheeseburgers, and drinks. Beth, however, wasn't her usual jolly self.

"I miss our 'spilling' tree Benny. We solved lots of problems under that tree, didn't we?"

asked Beth.

Benny picked up her hand that lay on the table. "Let's pretend that table in your room is our 'spilling tree' tonight. We will work this out together, Beth. I really think that your ideas on such a venture are what they want to start with, don't you?"

"I thought so, too, when I was talking to Mr. Brewster, but now I keep remembering him stressing 'the Board' and I think that he isn't sure of their acceptance," said Beth with a worried frown.

"Stop that, Beth, and relax while you eat," said Benny rubbing the top of her hand with his thumb. Beth looked down and thought, *that is such a comforting feeling*, but she moved her hand and Benny released it.

"I think I'd better eat and get back to the room, so let's not start a conversation. I don't have time for discussions, right now," said Beth.

Benny nodded his head at Marlo. "She's not going to listen to me, Marlo, so we may as well wolf down our food, or she'll leave without us."

Marlo giggled as she ate her last French fry. "I've already been a wolf, Benny. See, mine's all gone."

Benny smiled and thought, *Marlo is a beautiful young woman, but she is like a child in lots of ways. I hope some man doesn't take advantage of her innocence.* He put down his napkin and looked at Beth who was rising from her seat.

"I guess we're all finished, or I hope we are, for Beth has decided it is time to leave," said Benny giving Beth a tender smile, but she looked away.

When they reached their rooms, Benny stopped before their doors were opened and said, "Why don't you girls get ready for bed, and I'll do the same. We can work as well in pajamas and robes as we can in street clothes. We'll just be more relaxed."

However, by ten o'clock, Marlo was sleeping soundly, but Beth and Benny were writing, discussing, and then erasing.

Finally, at midnight, Benny yawned and said, "I'm through with this, Beth. I just don't have another thing to add or take away, so I'm going to leave and try to get some sleep. You should too. If you had all the points covered and fell asleep while talking, you would not impress anyone."

Beth looked up at Benny and smiled. She yawned as well and rose to her feet. "Yes, go on to your bed, Benny. You've helped me enough."

Suddenly, her eyes blared widely. "Benny, you have that test tomorrow!! Oh, Benny, I'm so sorry. I shouldn't have allowed you to stay up half the night to help me. I'm not being much of a friend and I'm so ashamed."

Benny grinned sleepily. "Well, if I don't pass, I can always blame you and then I won't feel so stupid."

Beth went to the door and opened it. "Get yourself out of here and into your bed. What time do you need to leave in the morning?"

"I'll have time to take you down to breakfast. The test is at ten o'clock and it shouldn't take more than ten or fifteen minutes to get there," said Benny as he went out the door.

Beth stepped into the hallway and Benny turned when he reached his door. "Breakfast is provided here, and it is added to the bill, so you don't need to stay awake and count your money again."

Beth smiled and went back inside and closed her door. She realized she was too tired to do anything else and went to bed as well. She thought she wouldn't sleep, but Benny's knock on the door, at seven-thirty the next morning, startled her to wakefulness.

She jumped out of bed and ran to the door saying, "Who is it?"

"Time to get up, Beth. I knew you didn't have an alarm clock and the front desk called me," said Benny.

"Okay, thanks! I'll get Marlo up and we'll be ready by eight o'clock," replied Beth in a sleepy voice.

# CHAPTER 30

The three of them trooped downstairs to the hotel dining room and found that a continental breakfast was to their liking. "This is the kind of breakfast I like, Benny. Do you suppose they serve this kind of breakfast every morning?" asked Beth.

"I think so since it was like this in the hotels where our team stayed when we traveled to away ball games," said Benny as he took his last drink of coffee and rose from his seat.

Beth was finished and arose, and Marlo was already on her feet, but she left with a banana in her hand. Benny saw it and grimaced. *She sure is like a child, but anyone who doesn't know her will only look at her pretty face,* he thought with a worried frown.

Nothing was said until they reached their rooms and then Beth stopped in front of Benny. "Marlo and I will be praying for you, Benny. I know you will do well and will soon leave us for Morgantown. I hate to see you go, but I want what is best for you."

"Hush! Don't talk about that or you'll make me sad. I'll really mess up if I go in there blubbering like an idiot," said Benny trying to smile.

You're too big to cry, Benny. Big boys don't cry. They cuss," said Marlo in a hard voice.

Benny looked at Beth and grinned. "If I

don't get a move on, I may cuss, so I wish you well also, Beth. I know you'll do great. I'll see you this evening." He reached out and patted Beth's cheek and quickly turned away. Beth stood watching him until he entered the elevator and was gone from sight. Beth turned back into the room with a sigh.

From then until they went out for lunch, Beth silently rehearsed her presentation, but Benny interrupted her rehearsal.

*Lord, please help Benny to make a high score. He is such a good person and has been my best friend,* Beth silently prayed every few minutes.

Finally, at one o'clock, they decided to go to McDonald's for lunch. "We'll stay out until four o'clock since it will be two o'clock by the time we've finished lunch," said Beth, and Marlo eagerly agreed.

"Let's walk around and look in the shop windows, Beth. I know we can't buy anything, but I like to look at pretty things." That's what they did until three o'clock and then turned down the street that led to the law offices.

Soon Beth and Marlo arrived at the Brewster, Pendleton, & White offices and rode the elevator to the second floor. Beth was nervous and scared yet tried to hide it from Marlo, who was also scared.

"Do you think that Miss Jackson will be

friendly, Beth," asked Marlo as she brushed her hair.

"I think she'll be nice Marlo, but she can't sit and chat or she would lose her job. So, promise me that you won't worry her with chatter. You have that Anne of Green Gables book, to read while you wait for me," said Beth as she clutched her key, the legal pad, and her handbag.

As they rode the elevator, Beth was anxious about her interview, but she was silently praying for Benny. *Please, Jesus, let him make a high score on that test. Benny is too smart to just take any kind of job. He wants to work at something that will help people and research would be ideal for that. I'll miss him so much and perhaps I'll never see him again.* Her prayer stopped there since she felt tears in her eyes.

She angrily brushed her hand across her eyes and looked ahead to the offices of Brewster, Pendleton, & White Attorneys at Law. She clenched her teeth, took a deep breath, squared her shoulders, and stepped out of the elevator.

As soon as she opened the office door, Nancy Jackson was waiting for her. "Good evening, Miss Riley, you're here a little early. Does that mean you are eager?"

Beth smiled. "Yes, and no. I want to get through this even though I'm a nervous wreck, and I sure did not want to be late."

She looked at Miss Jackson for a moment and then asked, "Would you mind if Marlo sits out here and reads her book while I'm being interviewed? I didn't want to leave her in the hotel alone and Benny had to take his test today."

"You have a real friend there. Benny called me this morning to make sure it was all right. I think he would have chucked the test if I had said no. Marlo and I will get along fine. I may take her down to the deli later this evening if that is all right with you," said Nancy.

Beth sighed and said, "Sure, Marlo can go with you. Does she need any money?" Miss Jackson explained that the company always paid when someone was being interviewed.

"That's good, but Marlo isn't being interviewed," said Beth opening her purse.

Miss Jackson shook her head. Marlo is a part of the deal, so don't worry. I think we should concentrate on praying for Benny."

Beth nodded with a smile. "Yes, we need to pray for Benny. He is and always has been my best friend. I appreciate any prayers for him, and I know he will appreciate them also."

The door behind Miss Jackson's desk opened and Mr. Brewster put his head around the door. He smiled when he saw Beth and came on into the room.

"I see you came a little early and that is

good since employers like promptness in their employees. Some of the board members aren't here yet since some of them travel several miles to get here," explained Mr. Brewster as he stood studying Beth.

"I hope I'm dressed appropriately, Mr. Brewster. It is the most professional-looking outfit that I own. In fact, I've been so worried about this project that nothing else has been on my mind except this project and Marlo, of course." Beth realized she was talking too much and suddenly stopped.

Mr. Brewster looked back through the door into his office and then turned back. "I think they are all here, Beth, so if you are ready, we may as well go in."

Beth looked at Marlo and murmured, "Remember, Marlo. You can talk but when Miss Jackson is busy or someone is talking to her, you stay quiet and read your book."

Marlo smiled and whispered. "I promise, Beth," and walking behind Mr. Brewster, Beth left the room.

Marlo read her book halfway through and went down to the deli with Miss Jackson, where they purchased milkshakes. When they arrived back in the office, Beth had not returned.

Marlo was, at first, uneasy, but it got worse as the evening advanced. When the clock in a nearby church tower chimed five times, Marlo raised frightened eyes to Miss Jackson. "I'm scared! It is five o'clock and it is almost supper time. What has happened to Beth?"

Miss Jackson saw the frightened look on Marlo's face and thought, *this girl has a problem and I hope she doesn't get out of control. I see why Beth is so careful and concerned about leaving her alone.*

These kinds of interviews always last a long time, Marlo, but I'm sure they have been good to Beth. So, don't get upset. Beth will soon be finished and then the two of you can go eat or whatever you want to do together.

# CHAPTER 31

At six o'clock Mr. Brewster's door opened, and Marlo jumped to her feet. When she didn't see Beth, she gave Mr. Brewster a wild look. "What have you done to Beth?"

Mr. Brewster looked startled for a moment and then realized that Marlo was truly scared. "She is in the restroom, Marlo. She'll be out in a few minutes."

Marlo's eyes were full of tears and when Beth stepped into the room, she rushed toward her with her arms wide. "Oh Beth, I've been scared to death. It is six o'clock and you went in there at four this evening."

Beth hugged Marlo. "Sh-h, it's all right, Marlo. I'm here and we can go back to the hotel."

"Supper! You didn't get to eat supper, did you?" asked Marlo, giving Mr. Brewster an angry glare.

"We fed her, Marlo. The caterers brought food up from a restaurant and we gave her a good supper, didn't we, Beth?" asked Mr. Brewster with a gentle smile at Marlo.

Beth stood patting Marlo's back for a moment and then moved back so she could look at Marlo. "Oh yes, I had baked salmon, green beans, creamed potatoes, a salad, and a delicious dessert." She rubbed her stomach and smiled.

Marlo still held onto Beth's hand, but she was much calmer as she looked at Miss Jackson.

"Beth saved me, and she takes care of me. I get scared when she leaves me; especially when she stays away so long."

Mr. Brewster looked at Miss Jackson with raised eyebrows, but Beth did not see him. He walked over to Miss Jackson's desk and then turned to Beth.

"We've not officially voted yet, but I feel confident that you made a good impression. We will not know for sure until Monday, so Nancy . . .Ms. Jackson. . . will give you an expense card so you will have funds for the next two days."

Beth looked astonished. "I don't . . . I mean, how will you be repaid if I'm not hired?"

Suddenly she looked at Mr. Brewster and said, "I'd forgotten about it, Mr. Brewster, but I may have some money. I have no idea how to tap into it. My father worked for the U.S. Steel Corporation in Pittsburgh, Pennsylvania, and when he was killed, the company set up some kind of trust fund or something for me. I don't know much about it, but I received $25.00 a month to pay for anything I needed. Mr. Wright told me I would not receive the rest until I graduated or was twenty-one years old. Since I have graduated, do you think I could get it now," Beth asked.

Mr. Brewster's eyes lit up and he said, "I don't know, Beth, but I will certainly find out for you. It probably depends on the wording of the trust, but I'll check it out. I know a man who has connections to U. S. Steel, but it may take some time to track him down."

"I still want to work and go to college regardless of whether I can get anything or not. I just thought that right now, if I had a little money, I could look for a place for Marlo," said Beth with a troubled look on her face.

Miss Jackson handed Beth a card and said, "Here you are Miss Riley, or may I call you Beth?" Beth nodded with a smile.

"Yes, I wish you would, and I'd like to call you, Nancy. Is that all right, with you?" asked Beth.

"Yes, you may, Beth, so get that worry out of your mind," said Nancy as she handed Beth a credit card. "You can eat in the Hilton dining room if you wish, for the next few days."

Marlo's eyes lit up. "Can we take Benny, too? He's been so good to us." She looked at Beth, "He has been good to us, hasn't he, Beth?"

Beth smiled at Marlo. "Yes, Marlo, Benny has been a good friend."

Mr. Brewster chuckled as he looked at Marlo. "Sure, we don't want Benny to starve, do we?"

Beth put out her hand. "Thank you, so much, Mr. Brewster. I'm so glad I've met you and I'll still feel that way whether I'm hired or not."

Mr. Brewster shook her hand and said, "I

feel the same way, Beth, and I'm sure Nancy feels the same." He looked at his secretary and she smiled.

"Oh yes, they've both been a pleasure to know; especially Marlo, who is such a help with shopping. We had a good time, didn't we, Marlo?" asked Nancy.

Marlo looked at Miss Jackson with shining eyes. "Yes, it was lots of fun and I had a chocolate milkshake. Beth, you need to get a milkshake. It is the best drink I've ever had in my whole life."

Beth chuckled. "Okay, you've talked me into it, Marlo, but I don't really like chocolate."

"They make strawberry shakes, and lots of other kinds, don't they, Nancy?" said Marlo, looking around to see if she had permission to call Ms. Jackson, Nancy.

"They sure do, Marlo. You'll have to get Benny one as well," said Nancy as she thought, *that sweet innocent child/woman, I sure hope God watches out for her.*

After assuring Mr. Brewster that she would be there again on Monday morning at ten o'clock as the board had requested, Beth and Marlo left the office.

When they arrived back at their room, Benny's door opened before Beth could unlock her door. "Did you get the job, Beth?" were his first words.

Beth shrugged. "I don't know, Benny. I'll

find out at ten o'clock Monday morning though."

"Did you do well on your test? I've had you on my mind, off and on, all day," said Beth giving him a steady look.

Benny also shrugged. "Monday is D-day for me as well. I don't have to go back to the University here, but WVU will call me sometime Monday."

Beth unlocked their door and then said, "Have you had dinner, yet?"

"Nope! I was waiting on you two. I don't want to eat alone, do you? Of course, you have Marlo, but I don't have anybody," said Benny trying to look pitiful.

"You got me, and Beth, so you can eat with us. Beth has a card, and we can eat in the biggest hotel in town," chirped Marlo and then added, "We can have milkshakes if we want one. Beth doesn't like chocolate. Do you like chocolate, Benny?"

Benny looked at the big smile on Marlo's face and said, "Yum, yum! I can't wait. Hurry Beth and do whatever you have to do and let's go eat."

They didn't go to the biggest hotel in town, but the Radisson looked big enough and it was near enough to walk to since they were all hungry. They had a good meal and Marlo did get a milkshake.

"Don't you want to try a milkshake, Beth?

They are so good and I'm sure you will like them. They make strawberry shakes," urged Marlo.

"I'll try one, Marlo. I just don't want one tonight. Maybe I'll get one for lunch tomorrow," said Beth, and Benny nodded which seemed to please Marlo.

They strolled along the street on which the hotel was located, looking in the shop windows and discussing what they would buy if they had the money.

Beth suddenly put her hand on Benny's arm. "I may have some money coming to me, Benny. Do you remember me telling you about the $25.00 I received every month?"

Benny listened as they strolled along while Beth explained what Mr. Brewster had told her about U.S. Steel and the trust that had been set up for her after her father was killed.

"Mr. Brewster said that he knew somebody connected to U.S. Steel and that he will check it out. He thinks there may be a good sum of money accumulated."

He talked like he would have no problem finding out if there is a trust and if so, how to access it," said Beth with a happy smile.

# CHAPTER 32

Benny smiled. “I don’t know if I’ll know how to react to an heiress. I’ve always liked Beth Riley just as she was when I stuttered.”

Beth looked up at Benny. “That was hard for you, wasn’t it?”

“Not after you came along ready to do battle with the first person who laughed at me,” said Benny, giving her an intent stare.

Beth laughed. “I’m sure you felt a lot safer since I weighed about sixty pounds, didn’t I? I must have looked mean though for they quit being so quick to put you down. Of course, it was probably because they realized that you were more intelligent than anyone else in the class.”

“Not after you poked your fiery little head into the fifth grade. I don’t think they knew how to treat either of us, so they tried to put us both down. I suppose it made them feel good about themselves,” said Benny.

Beth shook her head. “No, I don’t think their thought processes were on that level. They acted just like everybody does about people and things that are different. It seems to be about conformity; you know, wanting everybody to think and act the way that ‘they’ think people should.”

“You’re probably right. People march and do all kinds of dangerous things that are not helpful to anybody, but they vandalize and ransack whole areas and the taxpayers have to do the reconstruction," surmised Benny looking very solemn.

"Beth, you said that you would march with Martin Luther King and all those black people," spoke up Marlo.

"Yes, I did, Marlo, and I meant it. That was a march for equal treatment and those marchers were peaceful. That was their way of gaining public attention to the injustice done to so many of the Lord's people. That was a true 'freedom of speech' march, and it brought about change," stated Beth with a quickened step.

Benny laughed. "You look ready to march, Beth. Thank God for the change and I'm thankful that there are still people in this country that understand that human beings are not perfect. Some truly awful things have happened to and against humanity, in all races, all cultures, and all ethnic groups. However, when there are enough people who realize that there is great pride in their endeavors, a group of people can improve their lives in peaceful and meaningful ways. When people like Dr. King help to bring attention to the wrongs by letting the public see for themselves, then the goodness in 'the majority' of the people, comes to the forefront and great change for the better occurs."

"Hear, hear! This man has a message: Friends, Romans, Countrymen lend him your ear," said Beth, stopping to salute.

Two ladies who were walking down the other side of the street stopped and stood watching them until Benny nudged Beth. "You are attracting an audience, Beth. I think we'd better take our rallying cry to the hotel."

Beth turned red and walked a little faster until they were nearing their hotel. Benny noticed her embarrassment and said, "Beth, don't be upset because you are an advocate for justice even if it is only to discuss it. I think we should be thankful that we are smart enough to see the 'big picture' and we do care."

They got to their room and Benny went into his room but turned at the door. "If we had a jigsaw puzzle, it would be an enjoyable way of spending some time, wouldn't it?"

"We don't have one, so I guess we'll have to think of something else, or you could go down to the Five and Dime Store. I saw one on the corner of this same street," said Beth with a questioning look in her eyes.

Benny nodded as he shut his door and turned toward the stairs.

Beth looked up with startled eyes when the clock on the Presbyterian Church across the street chimed twelve times. She looked at Benny who sat with a puzzle piece in each hand.

"You don't have a free hand to fit those pieces in place, so what are you doing?" she asked.

Benny smirked. "I have the honor of solving this puzzle. Nobody but me can do it. I'm just waiting for a drum roll."

"Those twelve chimes are your drum roll. I'm tired and you can roll yourself back to your room so we can get a few hours of sleep," ordered Beth rising from her chair and stretching.

Benny arose and stretched as well. "I can't believe that we are here, Beth. Did you ever in your wildest dreams ever imagine us doing what we've done in the last few days?"

Beth smiled. "No, Benny, I think that all the years I lived at Mountain Mission School I felt like . . . like my life was on hold or something. I just wanted to learn and find my place in the world. Does that make sense?"

Benny shrugged. "That's deep water, my friend. I only thought about how to stop stuttering for a long time."

"It seems like you only did that for the first year after they moved me into the fifth grade," said Beth.

Benny smiled at her and said, "I think that's another reason I love you so much, Beth."

"Now you're talking out of your head. You need some sleep, my friend, so get out of my room. Your bed awaits you," said Beth opening the door to urge him out.

Benny went and she didn't see him again until lunchtime the next day when they met to go out for lunch.

Marlo had awakened Beth at eight o'clock wanting to go down for breakfast. When they finished breakfast, Marlo wanted to walk around and they explored their street and the next street over. On that street, they found a pizza parlor and, being curious, they went in and bought two pieces of pizza.

"Um, this is good Beth. How do you say its name again?" asked Marlo.

Beth laughed. "I listened to that man. He said 'pete-za' like it had a T in its name, but it isn't spelled like that, is it? I think we have a lot to learn Marlo."

# CHAPTER 33

Monday morning finally arrived, and Beth was eager to get back to the law offices. Benny, however, had to sit and wait until West Virginia University called him.

"Benny, don't you leave before I get back. I want to know where you'll be going. I want to keep in touch, don't you?" asked Beth.

Benny smiled, sadly. "I'm glad you're so optimistic. I may be staying here and part of me hopes I will. Do you realize that we have been best friends for thirteen years? Beth, I don't know if I can bear to not see you every day."

Beth chuckled. "Well, you went whole weeks without seeing me when Mr. Scales was doing construction, and we couldn't even write to each other. You'll be getting so many letters that you'll tell the post office to stop delivering them."

"That'll be the day! I know how you hate to write letters, Beth, so I'll not be expecting to be deluged with mail," said Benny, and Beth who knew Benny so well and saw that he was getting emotional, looked at her watch.

"Gosh! we'd better get started or all of us will be stuck here without a place to stay, and I don't want that. You get back to your room and get all your stuff together, Benny, for I know that you passed that test with flying colors. You can tell me all about it when I get back this evening," said Beth as she turned to Marlo.

"You get to stay with Nancy again, so I guess that means another milkshake, doesn't it?" Marlo licked her lips.

"Um, yum! I hope she takes me to that same place today.

Soon they were all ready and left their rooms at the same time and walked down the stairs together. As they walked out the door, Benny put his arm around Beth's shoulder and pulled her toward him.

Beth pulled away and looked up at him, "You don't need to hug me, Benny. I'll see you this evening. You put your head up and walk tall and proud because you are going to do well . . . I honestly believe you will, Benny."

Benny dropped his arm and said, "If you're right then I'm going to hug you, my friend, whether you want me to or not."

Beth laughed. "I guess that means I'll have to punch you out, since you know I don't like hugs from men."

They both turned their separate ways and Marlo impulsively hugged Benny, before turning away with Beth as she said, "I believe in you, too, Benny, and I don't care if you want to hug me."

Beth walked into the reception area of the Brewster, Pendleton, & White Law Offices at nine-fifty and Nancy looked up with a smile. "I knew you wouldn't be late, so I've brought you a mocha coffee. You'll need the caffeine before this day is done, and I brought my new friend, Marlo, a chocolate milkshake and a Danish."

Beth had never had mocha coffee before, but she said, "Thanks! I hope I get to work here, so I can take you to lunch someday. Otherwise, I don't know how to repay your kindness."

Nancy turned with a big smile on her face. "If everybody feels like Mr. Brewster does, I'll be getting that lunch pretty soon."

"I hope you're right, Nancy, but there are eight other people on that board, and they did not know I existed until Friday," said Beth as she took her first sip of mocha coffee. She drank and swallowed and then looked up with a pleased expression.

"This is so good! Thanks for bringing it to me. I'm beginning to realize that there are many wonderful surprises awaiting us, Marlo. We're going to become educated, little sister," said Beth before taking another drink.

The clock in the Presbyterian Church chimed out and Beth turned pale. "It's ten o'clock. You girls pray that the board members are willing to hire me," said Beth just as the door to Mr. Brewster's office opened.

"Well, you will get praise for your promptness, Beth. Are you ready for our meeting?"

Beth drew in a long breath. "As ready as I'll

ever be, I suppose."

She turned to Marlo. "Remember your promise, Marlo and don't disturb Nancy."

Marlo smiled. "I won't, Beth. I promise."

Beth smiled at Mr. Brewster. "Lead the way, Sir."

Mr. Brewster turned back into his office and on through another door that led to a large conference room with a long table and chairs in the center. Beth followed him in and stood waiting.

"Good morning! As you can see, Beth Riley was early. That is one of the criteria that Gilbert stipulated, so we can mark that one off."

Mr. Brewster went to the head of the table and Beth followed. He pointed to the seat at the head of the table and said, "This will be your seat during this interview, Beth." Beth smiled and took her seat.

When everyone was seated, Mr. Brewster arose and looked around the room.

"Gentlemen, we all know why Beth Riley is here, so if it is agreeable with her, and with all of you, I think Miss Riley, or Beth, should tell us what she thinks this position should entail. Once she has finished, then taking turns, each board member may feel free to ask any questions pertaining to the position. Is that agreeable with everyone? Silence can show agreement if you so desire."

When everyone nodded but remained silent, Mr. Brewster smiled and said, "Beth, the floor is yours."

Beth swallowed as she rose to her feet. "Good morning, gentlemen. I wish to thank you for this interview. I have thought about this position the entire weekend. I've made a list of what I think should be in a curriculum to produce lawyers who are qualified and capable of handling any case that comes before them." Beth stopped, swallowed, and then drank from the water provided before continuing.

"Anyone aspiring to be a lawyer needs to be skilled in public speaking so a curriculum should have classes in all kinds of speaking as well as several classes in debating. Therefore, those classes are first on my list. The university may already offer those things, but as you recall, I wasn't allowed to see what was already offered."

Beth stopped and stooped to lift a tote bag from the floor where she had placed it when she first entered. She then turned to face the group. "I have copies of everything that I thought would be of benefit to a law student. Rather than go over each item, I felt that you would have the opportunity to review my ideas and then we could discuss my reasons for each concept. If each of you wanted to hear about a particular class that I have listed, we could cover each one with more time for discussion of each issue."

She looked around the table and asked, "Is this acceptable or do you wish to continue as we started?"

An older man seated near the end of the table spoke up. "I'm Kenneth Callebs, and I think this is better, as you said, and it will take up less time. If the others agree, I'll help you pass those out and then we can break for lunch."

# CHAPTER 34

This process worked to the satisfaction of everyone, but even with that, Beth was not released until four-thirty. As she closed her tote preparing to leave, Mr. Callebs said, "I'm satisfied with Miss Riley, but the board will need to vote."

He looked at Beth and asked, "Will you come back tomorrow morning at ten o'clock for our decision, Miss Riley?"

Beth smiled and agreed. *I guess that some of these men are not on board, and I may not be hired. I'm so tired and stressed out that right now, I don't really care,* she thought as she picked up the now empty tote and left the room.

Nancy's office was empty, and Beth looked around the room with a startled gaze. She turned to go back and ask Mr. Brewster just as the outside door opened.

Marlo came through the door and her eyes lit up at the sight of Beth. "You're finished! Good! Guess what I've been doing?"

Nancy came in behind her and she was also smiling. "Marlo has been to a pet store, and I think she is in love with a little black and white kitten. I had to threaten her by telling her you would leave without her if we didn't hurry back."

Beth looked at Marlo with a grimace. "Marlo, I don't know whether I have a job or not, and we don't have a place to live, so don't start begging for a kitten."

"But, Beth, it doesn't have anybody to love it, and it came right to me when I stopped to look at the kittens," said Marlo with a soul-wrenching look in her eyes.

Beth was tired and anxious and now Marlo would worry her frantic with pleas for the kitten. In exasperation, she spat out a harsh "NO!"

Marlo gasped in surprise. "Beth! You've never spoken to me like that before. I wasn't going to get it right now, but I wanted to tell you how it loved me just like I loved it."

Beth looked at Marlo's astonished expression and regretted her reaction, but she still looked at Marlo, with tired, weary eyes, and said, "Marlo, this has been a trying day and I really don't want to discuss anything else. Let's go back to the room. We can talk about this some other time."

Nancy looked at Beth with compassion and wished she hadn't taken Marlo to the pet shop.

*I just want to get back to the hotel and see if Benny is there. When he leaves, I'll probably not see him again and I'm going to miss his friendship so much,* she thought as she steered an unhappy Marlo out of the office.

Benny, however, was there waiting for her in the lobby. Seeing Beth's tired walk and sad expression, he hurried to meet her as she entered the door. "What's wrong, Beth? Didn't you get the job?"

Beth headed for a seat along the wall and Benny followed with Marlo slowly following. Once seated she said, "I don't know Benny. One of the board members, Mr. Callebs, said he was completely satisfied, but that the board would have to vote, and they wanted me to come back tomorrow at ten o'clock for their decision. I could have waited if they would have voted this evening, but somebody must have been dissatisfied."

Benny sat down beside her and picked up her hand. "Beth, you know that Mr. Brewster has the final say, and he likes you, so if there is only one hold-out, I think you will still be hired."

Beth's expression lightened as she looked at Benny. "Mr. Brewster wasn't there today, so do you think he will go to bat for me?"

"I'd be very surprised if he didn't, Beth. He and I talked when we were bringing in the luggage. What he said about his meeting with you at Mountain Mission School made me think he was very impressed with you."

Beth nodded tiredly. "Well, I've waited this long, so surely I can handle one more day of waiting."

She pulled her hand from his clasp and said, "What about you, Benny? When do you leave?"

I have a ticket for nine in the morning. I'll

be staying in the dormitory, I suppose. However, if I can find some work, I'll try to get my own place. I've had enough of dorm living to last me a lifetime," said Benny turning to Marlo who had tapped him on the shoulder.

Marlo spoke up in an angry voice. "I was going to show you my kitten, but Beth threw a fit when I started to tell her about it. Now, somebody else will probably buy it before I can go back to the pet shop."

Beth rose to her feet and so did Benny. "Come on, Marlo, and we'll go to our rooms and talk about this. Beth has enough to worry about right now," said Benny grasping Marlo's hand and pulling her to her feet.

Attention from Benny is all that Marlo needed to forget about being sad. "Okay, Benny, I'm not mad at Beth anymore. She's had a rough day."

*It takes so little to please Marlo,* thought Beth and grinned as she thought, *too bad I'm not a man when she gets into a snit.*

They all went to Beth's room and by seven o'clock, Benny had revealed that he would be bound to Morgantown and the university for several years. "It depends on the demands this scholarship makes on my time, Beth, but if it is possible, I'll come for a visit at Christmas. Will that be all right with you?" asked Benny.

Beth looked sad. "That's seven months

away. Surely you can have a free weekend before that, can't you?" she asked as she felt tears welling up in her eyes and quickly dashed them away with the back of her hand.

"You're not about to cry are you, Beth?" asked Benny in surprise since he had always thought that he cared more for Beth than she did him.

"Cry! Heavens no! What good would that do? Of course, I hate that you have to be so far away, but my eyes are just so dried out from all that stress and writing that I've been doing that I felt 'watery-eyed' for a moment,'" explained Beth.

Marlo came out of the bathroom. "Are we going out to eat? I'm hungry and it is seven o'clock."

They again went out to eat and while eating, they both promised to write. "I don't know what my address will be until I have a job," said Beth as she sat back in her seat.

"You can send your letters and hopefully a phone number as well, to the university," said Benny looking at the sadness on Beth's face.

"Beth, I feel confident about this job you're trying to get and hate that I can't wait to know for sure, but a four-year scholarship is a 'dream come true' for me. I don't want to mess up before it starts by not showing up," said Benny.

Beth tried to smile and said, "Please don't

be late, Benny. I'm so proud of you since research has been all you've talked about down through the years. I knew I wanted to go to college, but I wasn't certain what I wanted to go into, but you always knew."

So, the next morning Beth and Marlo walked with Benny to the bus station and hugged him as he got in line to board the bus. Marlo was crying and Beth crimped her lips together and tried to smile as he crushed her to him and hurriedly turned away and didn't look back.

# CHAPTER 35

Once the bus had pulled out, Beth and Marlo walked to Mr. Brewster's office. Marlo was still softly sniveling as she kept up with Beth's marshaled steps. *I hope Mr. Brewster is there this morning,* thought Beth as she turned to Marlo.

"Stop crying, Marlo, and wipe your eyes. I don't want them to think I beat you."

Marlo laughed but wiped her eyes with the tissue Beth handed her as they entered the street-level lobby of the law offices.

When they entered the door, Nancy looked up from her computer and smiled. "Mr. Brewster is eager to see you. Let me page him and then you can go right on in. Marlo can stay with me, and I promise not to take her near a pet store."

Beth smiled and stood waiting for a moment as Nancy paged Mr. Brewster. Nancy looked up from her computer and said, "Go on in, Beth. He's waiting on you."

Beth stepped through the door just as Mr. Brewster rose from his seat. He motioned Beth to a seat and then he said, "Good morning, Beth Riley, the heiress, as well as the College Liaison Officer, if she wants it. How are you feeling this morning?"

Beth's eyes widened in surprise. "What do you mean? I'm . . . I'm not an heiress. Why did you say that?" she asked in an incredulous manner.

"Beth, you asked about U.S. Steel sending you that small check each month. I contacted Mr. Helmandollar, my friend, who has a connection with U.S. Steel. He says there is a relatively large trust in your name waiting to be utilized when you are twenty-one. However, after I told him your story, he thinks that you can access it in some manner right now," explained Mr. Brewster.

Beth sat stunned into silence. Before she felt capable of asking anything else, Mr. Brewster said, "That makes me wonder if you still wish to be our College Liaison Officer. Are you still interested?"

*Jesus. Is this really happening? I came here with no job, no money, and no place to live. and now I have the means to fix all that and go to college as well. I don't deserve all this,* thought Beth as she sat as if in a daze, until Mr. Brewster asked, "Beth, are you feeling all right?"

She still looked dazed, but she asked, "Did I get the job, Mr. Brewster?"

"Yes, but I hope you can act pleasantly surprised when Mr. Callebs announces it in the meeting. I'm sorry you had to wait until this morning, but yesterday, Mr. Williams had another appointment, and he was already late when the board adjourned."

Tears of joy flowed down her cheeks, but she said, "I'm fine, Mr. Brewster. In fact, I'm better than fine. I don't know what to say or how to act, but I'll wash my face and make those men think I never dreamed this could happen, which is true," said Beth as she rose to her feet.

Beth made a very good impression, and nobody on the board would have thought by her reactions that she expected to be hired. Mr. Callebs spoke up, "Beth . . ., may we all call you Beth?" When Beth smiled and nodded, he said, "I may have an answer for you about where Marlo can stay while you work. Are you interested?"

This time, Beth didn't have to act. She was ecstatic since Marlo had been her greatest worry since that long-ago moment when she had seen Marlo's battered swollen face on the day she was brought to Mountain Mission School.

"Oh yes, Mr. Calebs, I do want to hear what you've found. What is it?" asked Beth, sitting forward on the edge of her seat.

"Mrs. Beulah Clark, on Fourth Street, owns and operates Clark's Boarding House. She only accepts people who have references and have jobs. I spoke to her and she has a separate room with its own bath which you and Marlo could have if Marlo is willing to help her run her business. Is that something you would be interested in pursuing?" asked Mr. Callebs in a cautious voice.

Beth sat back with a long sigh. *Oh Jesus, how can I ever thank you? All of this good happening in one day,* thought Beth as she looked around the room in an amazed manner.

She rose to her feet with a broad smile and looked at each man going around the table. Finally, she said, "I don't have words to express my thoughts and feelings right now. I wish to thank each of you, and I promise I will work harder than I ever have in my life to be the kind of employee you gentlemen deserve. I came here with nothing but a good education and a desire to work, but I had no idea how to begin since I have always had the care of Marlo foremost in my mind. You see, gentlemen, Marlo doesn't have anyone to turn to except me. I feel it is my duty to take care of her, so thank all of you so very much."

She stopped and turned to Mr. Callebs. "Do I need to get an appointment, or do I just go there?" asked Beth.

Mr. Callebs looked cautious for a moment. "I told her Marlo knew how to cook and clean. Can she do that?"

Beth smiled. "That's what she loves to do. She only needs someone to tell her what needs to be done and she'll do a good job. She is not a fancy cook, but I'm sure she would learn if someone gave her the recipe and encouraged her."

Mr. Callebs smiled. "That's great and I'm supposed to bring you both to see her at two o'clock today. Is that all right with you?"

"Mr. Callebs, you're an angel, at least to me you are, and I'll certainly be ready. Where shall we meet you?" asked Beth.

"Whoa there! You're getting 'the cart before the horse,' Miss Beth. This board is not through with you yet. You will have to be filled in on your job expectations, your reported endeavors, your salary, your insurance and health care, and anything else pertinent to the position. We'll have lunch catered again today, and then I'll take you and Marlo to see Mrs. Clark," said Mr. Callebs.

# CHAPTER 36

When Beth and Marlo left the law offices with Mr. Callebs, Beth had a good position with the Brewster, Pendleton, & White Law firm in Huntington, WV. She had health insurance, life insurance, and the option to buy stock in the company, along with several paid holidays throughout the year, and now she was going to find a place to live for herself and Marlo.

Beth looked at Mr. Callebs with a bright smile. "It's amazing that all this is happening, and all in one day. If Mrs. Clark finds us acceptable, Marlo and I are the most blessed two girls that ever lived."

Mr. Callebs grinned. "Well, you did say I was your angel! I guess I'd better not take all the credit, though, for my wife knew about Mrs. Clark, so she's more of an angel than I am."

Beth laughed. "I guess she's an angel also for you two have given Marlo and me a much-needed opportunity.

Mrs. Clark was a small dark-haired dumpling in stature and in kindness as well. Her pleasant smile made Beth and Marlo feel at ease from the time they were introduced.

After verifying that Marlo knew how to cook and clean, they decided on a price for their lodging. "I've never hired anybody in this manner before, so let's do some figuring," said Mrs. Clark with a chuckle.

It was decided that since Marlo would earn twenty dollars each day but would only receive fifteen dollars as her salary, then the other five dollars would go for rent.

"So, for the both of you to live here and with Marlo working, it will cost you thirty-five dollars each week for rent. You will also get free meals which is a big help, and in that sense, Marlo will be earning much more than twenty dollars each day."

"How does that sound to you, Marlo? You'll be helping me, and I will be helping you, and we both will be helping Beth. So, is that agreeable?" asked Mrs. Clark as her eyes twinkled merrily at Marlo.

They had all been sitting around a table in the Boarding House kitchen and now Marlo jumped to her feet and hugged Mrs. Clark. "Yes, oh yes. I like to cook and clean, but first, you'll have to tell me how and what you want me to do," said Marlo with a broad smile.

Everyone was satisfied and their luggage was brought from the storage at the law offices. Marlo and Beth moved into their new home that same evening.

"We'll have to go out and buy an alarm clock and bathroom items, Marlo, but not until tomorrow. Mr. Brewster said I didn't need to start work at the office until Monday of next week," said Beth as she hung her dresses in the only closet in the room.

When the clock on the Presbyterian Church steeple chimed seven times, both girls had their clothes put away and as instructed, they went down to the dining room for their dinner.

Their dinner was country cooking at its best and they both enjoyed it. They had their meal with the other occupants of the house: three middle-aged women and two men who were older, but they were all nice.

Two of the women were Becky Taylor, who worked in the hotel where they had stayed and Judy Crockett, who worked for Home Health. Fred Jacobs was a salesman for Hoover Vacuum Cleaners and Tom Archer was a typesetter at the newspaper office.

Mrs. Clark had given out all this information as she introduced Beth as an employee of the law firm of Brewster, Pendleton, and White and Marlo as her new assistant. "They are new to the city and I'm sure they would appreciate any advice any of you have that will help them both adjust to city ways," said Mrs. Clark as she sat down at the head of the table and bowed her head.

Thus began the pattern of their days for the next few years, but neither of the girls thought of that at the time. Beth looked around the table, and said, "Yes, there is so much we need to learn. We are from a very rural area and things that seem ordinary to you will be strange to us, so we truly would appreciate any advice you have to offer."

Becky Taylor spoke up. "Even though Marlo is pretty, she still won't have no trouble since she will be here with Mrs. Clark all the time, but a pretty girl like you, Beth, will be offered lots of things, but you just mind your p's and q's, and don't believe any of their offers."

Beth turned red but smiled as she said, "Thanks, Ms. Taylor. I don't intend to let a man get that close to me and I'm glad Marlo will be here with Mrs. Clark."

"How are you going to work in a law office and not meet men, Miss Riley?" asked Mr. Jacobs with a speculative beam in his eyes.

Beth put down her fork and sat silent for a moment. "I meant meeting men socially. I, of course, will have to talk to men about work, but I won't be going out with any of them."

Mr. Archer grinned. "I think you will make some young men in this town, awfully sad, but you're probably wise."

Beth was relieved when Mrs. Clark said, "Dessert anyone! It is fresh apple pie and ice cream."

Everyone seemed to have a sweet tooth since they all had dessert.

When they all rose from the table, Marlo

began scraping the plates and stacking them to be carried to the kitchen. Mrs. Clark smiled since she hadn't told Marlo to start her job that evening.

"Marlo, do you want me to wait down here for you until you are ready to go upstairs?" asked Beth.

Marlo laughed. "Nope, you go on. I like working with Mrs. Clark and I'll be fine."

# CHAPTER 37

Before the month was out, Beth was enrolled in Marshall University and had classes from eight o'clock in the morning until one in the afternoon. She hurriedly ate her lunch in the cafeteria and caught a taxi back to Mr. Brewster's office where she worked until five-thirty each evening.

Her university classes were the general studies for a freshman and Beth found them to be easy, but learning about case studies and trial procedures as she typed and listened to recorded trial data was more difficult. However, she enjoyed her evenings much more than she did the mornings since her mind was constantly challenged.

Marlo loved working for Mrs. Clark, whom she now called Beulah. "Beth, I made scones all by myself today. We served them at lunch today and none were left on the serving tray," said Marlo as she prepared for bed one night.

"That's great, Marlo. You have just what you always wanted, and I'm so happy for you," said Beth as she brushed her hair.

"Don't you like your job, Beth? You never do say anything about it," said Marlo.

"I'm not as happy as you are, Marlo, but I'm learning lots of things," said Beth thoughtfully.

Beth lay back and closed her eyes, but lay

thinking, *I feel like I'm suspended, sort of betwixt and between. I don't know what I really want, so I'm not unhappy. However, it's like I'm not where I'm supposed to be or something.*

Mr. Brewster had gotten her trust all straightened out and now Beth had no money worries. She, according to Nancy Jackson, was doing very satisfactory work for the law firm, and the lawyers were pleased.

As Ms. Taylor had said, she got many requests for dates and was made several offers, but she brushed those off and tried to stay friendly. She even had a ride to the university each morning with Mr. Archer since he went by the university on his way to work.

Beth received short letters every week from Benny, for the first three months and then they became twice a month and she had only received one this last month. *I've answered every letter so there must be something wrong with Benny,* she thought trying not to worry.

Finally, she wrote a letter and asked him outright if something was wrong. A month later, she received a long letter explaining that he had been chosen to work on a serious research project and didn't have time to write. Beth understood, but she was lonely and sad. She had always had Benny to talk things over with and now she had nobody at all. Marlo would have listened, but she would not have understood the problem.

Marlo was doing great, and Beth didn't worry so much about her anymore, neither did she have any worries about money, or her job, but the feeling of being 'suspended in time' grew steadily worse.

*Am I having what's called a 'nervous breakdown,'* thought Beth, as she worked through her days with a dogged determination, but not in a happy frame of mind.

She had grown to respect and admire Mr. Brewster and knew that he would help her personally if she should ask. She didn't need to be wary about unwanted attention from Mr. Brewster since he was more of a father figure, which was a great relief to her.

*I wish something would happen to break this shell I'm living in,* she thought and debated in her mind whether to speak to Mr. Brewster about this strange malaise in which she found herself.

Christmas came and went with no word or visit from Benny and Beth was more deflated than ever. In the presence of others, especially Marlo, Beth smiled and chatted as she conscientiously strove to do what was expected of her.

In April, when Spring Break occurred at the university, she stopped by Nancy's desk on the following Monday. "Nancy, is Mr. Brewster working in Huntington this week? If he is, I'd like to set up an appointment," said Beth.

Nancy gave her a penetrating gaze for a moment and then said, "He won't be back to this office until the first of May. Is there a problem? I'm sure Mr. Brewster would drive up here if he isn't somewhere out west in some meeting."

Beth smiled. "No, there's no problem on my end and I hope there isn't one on his end, either. There is just something I've been thinking about and would like to talk to him about it."

"Good! I mean it's good that nothing has gone wrong with your studies or your work. I know you're, 'burning the candle on both ends' but that seems to be your personality.

"Are you saying that I'm a 'workaholic,' Nancy? I guess I am, but I know what I'm doing at work and there's nothing else to do outside of work," explained Beth.

Beth and Marlo had become good friends with Nancy and her family so now, Nancy said, "Beth, whose fault is that? My husband has invited you and I've asked you numerous times to spend time with us, but you seldom do. There's a Main Street Festival in Charleston this weekend. Do you and Marlo want to go with us? We'd be glad to have you and Marlo gets along well with our girls. Why don't you forget about work and have some fun this weekend?"

Beth knew that Marlo would love it and

that she, herself, needed to do something different. She grinned at Nancy and asked, "What do we need to bring? Do we buy food there or take picnic food?"

"Maybe you should bring some quarters and dollar bills for somebody told me the prices had gone up at these kinds of events since last year," said Nancy with a satisfied look on her face.

So, the following weekend both Marlo and Beth did something different and they both thoroughly enjoyed themselves. Sunday night, Beth slept all through the night and awoke in the morning, feeling better than she had in weeks.

However, by the end of the day on Monday, the same feeling came back with a vengeance.

*"This doesn't feel like something is wrong, but what is it? It's like I'm waiting for something to happen, but that doesn't make sense. I'm not clairvoyant, or at least I'm not aware of it if I am,* thought Beth in bewilderment.

On Tuesday morning, she had made up her mind to talk to Mr. Brewster. She knew he was in Huntington and wondered why since, according to Nancy, he wasn't supposed to be there until May. She saw him go down the hall on Monday, but she had not spoken to him.

*He may think I'm 'losing it,' but I need to get rid of this awful emptiness or something*, thought

Beth as she stopped by Nancy's desk on the way to her office.

"Nancy, I saw Mr. Brewster yesterday. I thought you said he wouldn't be back up here until May," said Beth with a questioning look.

Nancy smiled widely. "Yes, he is here, and he will want to see you, I'm sure."

Beth looked puzzled. "Why would he want to see me? Have I done something wrong?"

Nancy shrugged her shoulders. "I'm not aware of any mistakes you've made but let me see if he is free right now. I know you've been wanting to talk to him." She punched the intercom button and told Mr. Brewster that Beth wanted to talk to him. She looked up with a smile. "He said, 'Send her in.'"

Beth crossed to his office door, knocked, then opened the door. Mr. Brewster was standing as if waiting for her and in a chair beside his desk sat a tall young man with wavy black hair and sparkling blue eyes. Beth stopped and turned a startled gaze at Mr. Brewster. "I'm sorry, Sir. Please forgive me. I thought you were alone."

Beth was mesmerized by those sparkling eyes and stood as if transfixed. *What is this?* she asked herself as she felt heat rushing into her face.

The young man seemed to be experiencing something as well since he didn't move either.

Mr. Brewster broke the spell as he said, "I wanted you to meet my nephew, Zane Douglas."

The young man jumped to his feet and Beth realized he was a lot taller than he looked while sitting down.

Mr. Brewster turned to him and said, "Zane, this is the girl I told you about, Bridget Elizabeth Riley, but we all call her Beth" Then Mr. Brewster turned to Beth with a smile. "Beth, this is my sister's son, Frederick Zane Douglas."

Zane walked toward Beth with his hand out and Beth put out her hand as well. "It is a definite pleasure to meet you, Miss . . . uh, may I call you Beth?' asked Zane and then stepped a little closer and asked, "Is that a Celtic locket?"

Beth put her left hand up and touched the locket. Her mother had placed it around Beth's neck when she left for the hospital and Beth had worn it every day since. She had taken it off only to bathe. She raised startled eyes to Zane's face.

"What did you call it? Why do you ask?" Beth questioned him since she had no idea what he was talking about.

Zane asked, "May I look at it a little closer? I believe that it is a true Celtic locket and if so, you have a very valuable piece of jewelry. Where did you get it?"

Beth dropped her right hand that she had offered and put that hand up to her locket. "My mother gave it to me when . . . uh. . . when I was four years old. It is valuable to me, that's for certain."

"Could you take it off so I can examine it more closely?" asked Zane in an awed voice.

Beth stood for a moment and then unclasped her locket and placed it in his hand. "Be careful with it. It is the most precious thing I have from my parents," explained Beth as she watched him closely examining her locket.

"It is . . . this is a real Celtic locket and there were only ten of these made. He did something and said, "See, it opens."

Beth gasped since she did not know that it opened, but she was further surprised when Zane said, "There's a piece of paper in it. May I take it out?"

He lifted out a very small, folded piece of paper, and said, "This is yours and I think it must be very important. You didn't know that the locket would open, did you?" he asked as he handed it to her.

Beth's hands were trembling so much that she had to will herself to be still, fearing she would drop it. Mr. Brewster saw the state she was in and said, "Beth, let me unfold it for you. You don't want to drop it."

Beth dropped it into his hand and stood like a statue when Mr. Brewster slowly opened the paper. It was so small that Mr. Brewster reached for his magnifying glass that he kept handy and turned to study the paper. It revealed a picture and the words *Bridwell Manor* and it was signed Agnes O'Riley.

Beth gasped and sank toward the floor, but Zane caught her and helped her to a chair. Mr. Brewster stepped to the door and told Nancy to bring him a coke. Then he turned back to Beth.

"That shocked you, didn't it, Beth? What does it mean to you?"

Beth looked stunned and didn't answer, but Mr. Brewster, persisted. "Does that mean anything to you, Beth? I mean the picture or the name Agnes O'Riley. Do they mean anything to you?" asked Mr. Brewster.

Nancy brought the opened coke in, and Mr. Brewster handed it to Beth. "Here Beth. Take a drink of this and try to pull yourself together."

Obediently Beth took a drink and then looked at the picture now spread on the desk in front of her. "I remember my father talking about how green Ireland was and how much he wanted Mom and me to see his home. He described a big house just like this one, but I don't recall him giving it a name."

"I know you were very young when he was killed, but do you remember him mentioning anyone named Agnes?" asked Mr. Brewster.

Beth sat in thought for a moment. "I don't remember him saying that name. He named me Bridget after his twin sister, who died when they were in their teens. He always smiled when he talked about Briddy. I didn't know until later that he was speaking about somebody named Bridget. One of my teachers told me that Briddy was probably his shortened version of Bridget."

"How did you know about being named after his sister if you didn't know her name?" asked Zane.

"I remember my dad saying, "My twin sister died and when you looked so much like her, I had to name you after her," said Beth with a smile. Then she continued, "Elizabeth was my mother's middle name, so I became Beth. When Dad and Mom both died, I think I just refused to think about either of them. I was in a coma for a while, but Mrs. Collins was like a grandmother and helped me adjust to being an orphan." Beth took another drink of the coke and sat as if in a deep study.

Mr. Brewster seemed to be deep in thought for a few minutes. "Beth, I think your father may have altered his name a bit when he came to America. What if his name was James O'Riley and for some reason, he didn't want anyone to know his real name? What if his name was really James O'Riley?"

An audible gasp of surprise burst from Beth, and she turned pale. Zane Douglas grasped her arm as he looked to Mr. Brewster for help.

Mr. Brewster grasped her other arm and

said, "Beth, I think you'd better just sit and try to relax. This is too much to take in all at once, isn't it?"

Beth sat as if stunned for a moment and then said, "Other than saying 'Briddy' was his twin, I don't remember hearing my dad say anything about his family except a sister that he called, 'Aggie.' Then her eyes widened as she said, "That's short for Agnes, isn't it"?

"Yes, it is," said Mr. Brewster and picked up the painting again to sit studying it. "Did he describe a house that looked like this?" he asked, lifting the painting into her view.

Beth studied it for a moment and then said, "Yes, he did. He said that Aggie painted a picture of our home," said Beth with an astonished gasp, pulling the picture closer. She studied it narrowly for a moment and then looked up as tears rolled down her face.

"Isn't it sad? If this Agnes O'Riley is my dad's sister, Aggie, she doesn't even know I exist?" Beth mumbled from trembling lips.

Mr. Brewster knelt in front of her and took her hands in his and looking steadily at her he said, "That's why your dad gave your mother that locket and why she passed it on to you, Beth. He knew that someday, you would want to find your heritage and this picture would help."

# About the Author

Adda Leah Davis is a McDowell County, West Virginia native who has now lived in Russell County, Virginia for more than twenty years and dearly loves the entire area. She is a retired elementary school teacher and counselor.

After retirement from the school system she wrote for two newspapers in McDowell County, started an oral history theater group, and was Director of Economic Development in McDowell County for six years. After moving to Russell County, she has written and published nineteen books.

Mrs. Davis has presented workshops on oral history, community development, leadership, and writing. She is energetic and enthusiastic about any project she starts and about life in general.

When first leaving her life in West Virginia, she was devastated; but today, Davis will tell you that hearts, like love, can expand as hers has because she now loves Russell County, Virginia and the entire area. The many friends and fellow writers that she has been blessed to meet and learn to love attest to this knowledge.

# Other Books By the Author

You can purchase Adda Leah Davis' books from Amazon or if you would like them personalized, you can order from her website: addaleahdavis.com

You can email Addie at addie2shoes@gmail.com if you would like any information on her books.

Her upcoming series is called The Celtic Locket Legacy. It is sure to be your next favorite read. The many friends and fellow writers that I've been blessed to meet and learn to love attest to this knowledge.

Made in the USA
Columbia, SC
26 November 2024

47640236R00137